FAREWELL NAVIGATOR

FAREWELL NAVIGATOR

STORIES BY LENI ZUMAS

 OPEN CITY BOOKS

New York

Printed in the United States of America

FIRST EDITION

Thank you to my teachers, friends, and family. I'm also grateful for generous support from Yaddo, Hedgebrook, and the Millay Colony.

Many thanks to the journals where some of these stories first appeared, often in slightly different form: "Farewell Navigator" in *New Orleans Review*; "Dragons May Be the Way Forward" in *Open City*; "Heart Sockets" in *Quarterly West*; "How He Was a Wicked Son" in *Carve*; "Thieves and Mapmakers" in *Stand*; "Waste No Time If This Method Fails" in *New York Tyrant*; "Handfasting" in *The Journal*; and "Blotilla Takes the Cake" in *So to Speak*.

Book design by Nick Stone

Library of Congress Cataloging-in-Publication Data
Zumas, Leni, 1972–
  Farewell navigator : stories / by Leni Zumas.
    p. cm.
  ISBN-13: 978-1-890447-49-6
  ISBN-10: 1-890447-49-8
  I. Title.
  PS3626.U43F37 2008
  813'.6—dc22   2008005955

OPEN CITY BOOKS
270 Lafayette Street
New York, NY 10012
www.opencity.org

08 09 10 11 12 13   10 9 8 7 6 5 4 3 2 1

For my mother

and

in memory of my father

CONTENTS

FAREWELL NAVIGATOR

We live with the lights off in a rot-walled house. In our yard the dogs wait and a tree drops plums. I stand with a basket. Enough catch and Black will make plum salad, plum pie. All summer we chew sugar till our teeth sting. In the winter we eat from jars, cold runny fruit, and the radio plays in the dark.

Too pretty for the looking, says Black about Blue.

Too fat for the fucking, says Blue about Black.

I watch Black peel fruit so fast the colors smear. Purple skin, yellow meat, silver knife: his fingers know where to go. He's gotten fat, our Black—thighs shuddering, belly enormous. Blue calls him Pudding and whispers to me: I'd love to fuck a man who doesn't wobble. She can't see me blush or the tears that end in my mouth.

Too smart for the schooling, says Blue about me. She says I don't need much more.

Black says he can tell Blue's a stunner by the space between her eyes—three thumbs apart. He can tell it too from how her lips feel swollen to his finger but have never swelled in their sweet sucking lives. You're so pretty I don't even need to look!

Am I, son? she asks, frowning. Am I pretty?

I shake my head and say, Yeah.

I have meetings with the counselor, who urges travel. His hands are stacked with bright brochures. He says no nearby colleges are good enough. He speaks of my gifts like boxes waiting to be unwrapped and would like to know what my parents have to say on the subject. After our meetings, I sit under a table in the library and eat the long skin spooling from a gash on my knee.

When I was first learning to talk they said, Son, what do you see? and held their eyelids open wide. I said, Blue. What do you see? And I said, Black.

My father's eyes are actually brown but I didn't have that word yet. He has never seen his eyes. My mother could look at hers till the age of eight. By accident she stabbed her face with a No. 2 pencil, tearing a hole for infection to find.

The dogs are Swim and Swam. They came to us fresh from seeing-eye school. They are brothers and gentle as nurses. They spend most of their lives lying on beanbags or dirt since my parents don't leave the house much anymore. I am the leaver, the taker, the bringer.

I know a kid whose mother and father came to America too late to learn English, and the kid is always translating. Their language is one almost nobody speaks. Every trip to the doctor, he is needed; every major purchase, he goes along. A while ago his older brother got lupus and the kid, eight years old, had to do all the talking at the funeral parlor—tell the undertaker which coffin they wanted, explain to his parents why it cost so much. He goes home straight from school, same as I do, except on the days when we don't. We tell them detention and our parents believe us, but we are sliding beers under our jackets at the gas station and racing bikes to the cliff.

A bowl of peeled plum skins, the radio loud, fungus blooming in cracks down the walls: this is us without lights. When Black makes supper, he needs nothing but fingers and tongue. He hurts himself, sure—blood in ribbons on the cutting board, ropy splashes on the ramekins—but not as often as you might think. He is the carefullest of our family, happy to know in advance where the blade will sink.

Last week at the supermarket I bought a baby cow stomach. Black boiled it to make a juice that curdles milk into cheese. There are a million things I wish they could get on their own, but at the top of the list are cow stomachs and prescription vaginal creams.

The kid is coming for supper. I warn him that our house is damp as an old ship's hold and there is nothing on the walls.

Not even clocks or your dumb drawings from first grade?
I shake my head.

The kid smiles. So you could hang up that poster of Amber Cherry with her *pussa* shaved and they wouldn't give a fuck?

No fucks are given at our house about shaved Ambers, or stuck-out tongues, or me coming to breakfast with *PENIS* written in lipstick across my bare chest.

Soon as he gets here, the kid starts to sneeze. He waves his arms, waters his eyes, makes a sound between hiccup and squeal. Mold! he shrieks. We go back outside and he takes a little bottle from his backpack. We wait on the dirt for the medicine to work.

11

When my parents hang their hands out, the kid is quick to grab them. What a treat, burbles Blue, to have a guest for once in a lifetime! Guests are not plenteous at our house, but she didn't need to let the kid know. Quite a firm grip you've got, she tells him. I notice she takes her time letting go.

The table is set, as usual, with fork knife spoon clustered left of each plate. It looks like children did it. The walls are blank. There are no candles. Blue says to the kid: Let me feel your face. The kid bends to her, obliging. She strokes the soft hairs near his mouth. My husband's got skin like bacon, she says.

The kid looks at me, then at Black, then away. I give Blue the finger but this fails to amuse my friend. He is pushing cubes of stomach-juice cheese across his plate.

Once the kid's gone home, I droop with the dogs on their beanbags. From the living room trinkles Blue's radio; from the kitchen, Black's dishes. I have a bad feeling I don't know the name for. I coax up the rubbery scab on my knee and pull till a piece comes free big enough to chew.

Before sleep I do a few pages from the only book I've ever read twice, the tale of a ship that gets doomed when its navigator falls overboard. Nobody else in the crew can tell what the stars mean. They veer off course, drift north and north and north into a field of ice. Before they know it, the ship is surrounded.

That kid, your friend, is he handsome?
I don't know.
Of course you do, says Blue.
Well, he's not ugly, I say.
Eye color?

I never noticed.

Then notice next time, she says.

The word I learned today is *grubble,* which means feel in the dark. It came in a poem. *Thou hast a colour; / now let me rowl and grubble thee: / blind men say white feels smooth, and black feels rough: / Thou hast a rugged skin: I do not like thee.*

My teacher stopped reading and nervously coughed. That's enough of that, he said, and I hated the fact that every last person in the room was picturing my parents grubbling their fall-down way around our fall-down house.

I report to Blue: Green.

She frowns.

The kid's eyes, I explain.

Good to know, she says.

Green is the name of the hair on the ground, says Black, stirring salt into hot plum broth.

Why don't you have him over again? says Blue. It's nice for you to have friends.

I can be friends with him at school, I say.

It's also nice for me and Pudding to enjoy your friends, she says. Did you ever think about *that?*

I tell the counselor I will enroll at the CC in town and next year transfer to a better school.

Lots of people tell me that, he says, then next year never comes.

His office is crowded with tentacled plants. They live in the window like pet monsters. I reach to rub one of the little waxy leaves.

Let me draw you a picture, says the counselor. You are standing behind the counter of the video store where you work thirty hours a week. You are magnificently bored. You have an associate's degree from the community college, where you were magnificently bored for two years straight. You still live at home—

Where they kind of need me, I point out. They're fucking *disabled* in case you forgot.

He looks at his hands for quite a while. I look at them too: chapped, veiny. Then he says, Groceries can be delivered. That includes dog food.

But what about in a blizzard?

They could stock up beforehand, he says.

Tidal wave?

The amount of help you could give *anyone* during a tidal wave is, frankly, negligible.

But what if Swim and Swam get attacked by a copperhead and my parents have to carry them on foot to town and it takes so long they die on the way?

When I was a baby, we strolled as a family up the main street. A man on the sidewalk patted my father's arm. You're the bravest people I will see today, he said. Or tomorrow, for that matter. All fucking year.

Thank you, I guess, said Black.

The man said, Can I drive you someplace?

No thank you, said Blue, our feet are fine. And she reached to pinch mine, dangling at her ribs in little socks. I don't remember this, of course, but I hear the story often enough. They tell themselves like a picture: young man clutching lead of guide dog, young woman clutching young man's sleeve, infant strapped to her back. That dog was named Lucy, after the patron saint of eye troubles, and died of a snakebite when I was four.

People only call you brave, says Blue, when they're glad they don't have your life.

The green-eyed kid accepts my invitation to spend the night. He swallows his allergy medicine in advance. We stock up on gas-station beers and drink them in my room. I apologize for no TV. We lie dizzy on our backs, watching the dark. The kid tells me he applied early to a college one thousand miles from here and last week, he says, an acceptance letter came.

Aren't you worried about going? I ask. I mean, with your parents having no English?

He says, Not that worried.

A bat screeches near the window. I sit up. The kid is gone, a stripe of moon across the sheet where his body was. Hello? I call into the night. The walls are wet on my palm. He isn't in the bathroom, or the closet. Downstairs, a strand of noise from the kitchen—Blue's voice. Please, she is saying. Oh please. Give me your hand.

Plum chutney comes up my throat. I swallow it down.

I don't think so, says the kid's voice.

Please touch me. Please, here—

I run in and hit the light. Yellow pours onto Blue, who is naked except for underpants. Her breasts look like puddles of dough. The kid is backed up against the stove, hands over his face, sweatpants—thank god—on.

What the fuck, I shout.

Shit, says Blue. She stoops to feel for her nightgown. She's feeling in the wrong direction, so I pick it up myself and throw it at her.

Farðu í rassgat! shrieks the kid. Then he says, I'm gonna go.

He runs out the kitchen door, barefoot. Gravel sprays up hard from the wheels of his bike.

•

I skip school for three days. I ride out to the cliff, lie on the dirt, and read about the doomed ship. My favorite part of the book is when the sailors line up on deck at midnight, pointing pistols at their own hearts. They've already shot the sled dogs for meat. They've already broken their eyes on the dazzling ice looking for birds and seals that weren't there.

On the third morning, I head downtown to sit on the bench in front of the post office. A column of little blind kids is snaking up the main street. They must be on a smell-the-countryside field trip from their special institution. A few of them wear sunglasses fastened with cord. A few have tiny white canes. Some are just plain and kid-looking, except for the fluttering eyelids. They skip and twist and wriggle, anchored fast to the hands of teachers. Despite their cuteness, I don't smile. How the hell can I be jealous? It's sick to be—but I kind of somehow am. They have the teachers' hands to pull them. Nobody expects them to know where to go.

The kid is at his locker, getting the book for math. I have his sneakers in a grocery bag. Here, I whisper.

He looks in the bag and nods. My feet practically froze off riding home.

I'm sorry.

It's not *your* fault, he says.

The college applications make a pile on my desk beneath the poster of Amber Cherry's bald *pussa*. Outside, the jars of plum jelly make a lonesome sound when they explode on the sidewalk. I pick them from the basket, one at a time, and hurl.

The screen door slams and Black comes charging across the yard, though it's not as much a charge as a cane-assisted waddle.

16

Son? Son? He smells me, hears me. Like a giant bat, he homes in. What are you breaking? He trips on a root and the dogs get to their feet, but he steadies himself.

Nothing you can't make more of, I yell.

The sidewalk is like a ship's deck after a battle at sea.

Please stop doing that, he says.

He cannot catch me. If he were to swing, I'd duck. If he were to lunge, I would dance away. But I don't move when he stretches his arms out, pulls my face to his neck. I am swooped into warm fat. Like a house of human pudding, he quivers around me.

Is there a mess? he whispers.

Pretty big, I say.

Then you'll get the broom, but first—how come? His hands on my shoulder blades feel big and good, a sweet pressure at the back of my lungs.

I don't know, I say.

Let me draw you a picture: me climbing the corrugated stairs of a north-bound Greyhound while my parents, bravely smiling, flanked by Swam and Swim, wave in the approximate direction of the bus.

You don't know, says Black, or you don't want to tell?

He puts fingers to my cheeks, grubbling for tears. His eyes are closed but I see on the red-streaked lids, as if they were maps, how much he doesn't care if my bloody snot glops down his shirt. I see how he will hold my shoulders hard and fast for as long as it takes me to stop crying and how I can, if I want, stay bandaged in the soft heat of him for hours, leaking brine, tethered by giant arms to the beat under his ribs till night comes and we're afloat on dark water, shivering together, hearing the cold get brighter and the waves slower, so slow they turn from liquid to ice— hushed meadows of frozen lather—and we are surrounded.

DRAGONS MAY BE THE WAY FORWARD

The year James Agee died, my mother was finishing high school. She could have read his obituary in the paper but she was probably dropping the needle onto a record instead. All those sock hops—a relentless schedule—meant a girl had to practice. Her legs are so swollen now they couldn't dance if you paid them. While watching her rocket program, she props the knurly white logs on a milk crate. Look, she yells, he's hanging in the blackness from just that tiny cord and what if it snaps?

I say from the next room: It's made of steel. It won't.

James Agee had a drinking problem. He slept around on all three of his wives. He was a socialist obsessed with Jesus. He criticized the government and other writers and his own failed self. By the time he died—of a stopped heart in a taxi, age forty-five—he was in every sense a stray.

And so smart you could hear his brain tick ten blocks away.

And so louche you could lick him off the bottom of your shoe.

It would be better if I didn't think about him. But I do.

My mother is blattering about grace and bravery. They have launched a new rocket and its astronauts are so graceful and brave. Her favorite channel shows their faces, miles above Earth in airless air. That one's a schoolteacher, she says. Far left—see? She's got guts, that teacher. Maybe she'll write a book about her adventures.

I was stretched on a towel in the backyard, fourteen and no friends, when I first read *Let Us Now Praise Famous Men*. When the page said, "And spiders spread ghosts of suns between branches," a nerve I'd never felt before throbbed between my legs.

She shoves her hairdo into my room: Shall I open a can?

It is not soup we are talking about. It is not beer or tuna. Tapioca is the canned good of choice in this house. You wouldn't think it was a great idea to pack pudding in tin, but they do, and my mother eats a few cans a night under the pretense that I am sharing them with her. Two bowls, two spoons, one mouth.

Some speck on the wafer of her brain tells her that this rocket is traveling *now*. It is not, says her brain, a space mission that took place in the early eighties, but in fact an event of today. As we learn about the astronauts, observe their watery movements in the capsule, my mother refers to their moods and personalities in the present tense. When she gets up—slowly, slowly—to make another cup of hot water, I see worms dance on the purpling backs of her knees.

A question from *Famous Men* is burnt onto the skin behind my forehead: "How was it we were caught?" I know a little about caught. I know enough. There is this house. There is my mother. There is until she is dead.

•

She loves to plump the pillows on her Ku Klux furniture. Each pringly tassel must fall just so. She doesn't sit on the sofa anymore; she will cause too big of a dent. She uses a folding metal chair. I go on the striped wingback, rest the dictionary on my thighs, and read aloud. Her ghouly eyes listen. Sometimes her mouth, on its way to the pudding spoon, says: Read that part again.

The word is *moxa,* I say, and here are your choices: a medieval fortified keep; a small instrument used to brush hair off the South American goose; a preternaturally skilled hoagie maker; or a flammable material obtained from the leaves of Japanese wormwood.

Hoagie is a disturbing word, my mother says.

You have ten seconds.

Well, she says, I don't know what hoagie means so how can I choose?

It means submarine sandwich. In other parts of the land.

Then there's that goose—

Five seconds, I say.

I'll go with flammable material.

Are you sure?

Ha! she says happily, knowing she's right, since on wrong guesses I never ask.

A chewy cackle from the bathroom and I find her crouched near—but not on—the toilet. Massive gray panties swarm at her feet.

What the fucking fuck?

Don't say fuck so much, she says. No wonder you'll die a virgin, filthy mouth like that.

And no wonder she will die beached, left to drown yelling in the tide.

21

•

The word is *umbelliferous,* which might mean: excessively war-like; belonging or pertaining to the *belliferae* family of plants, including parsley and carrots; carrying an umbrella; or that which feeds from the underside.

Hard one, she says.

I'll give you an extra five seconds.

Maybe umbrella, she murmurs. Maybe parsley.

Don't forget that which feeds from the underside, I say casually, proud of this phrase. It's one of my best ever. A long belly seamed with nipples and the sucking, splittering mouth—

She guesses umbrella.

Sorry, I say, *belliferae* family of carrots and parsley.

Oh, damn. That was my close second.

Kitchen, late morning, matching yellow bathrobes.

The poison lake is awake!

Stop shouting, I shout.

She says, The wedding announcements page is especially interesting today.

Who?

Two girls from your year at St. Pancreas. It's gotten me thinking—

Do you want more coffee?

About how lonely you must be.

I'm not, actually. Hand me your cup.

Of course you are, beechnut. And it's not your fault. Well, *some* of it is your fault, because if you don't leave the house how can you. . . . But some of it's just plain bad luck. You're unlucky in love.

No, I say, I'm just waiting.

Her mouth makes a sickle of *Go ahead and believe that.* Yes, mother, thank you, I will go ahead. Her haught is terrible, but when she dies, that chin won't jut any longer. Its meat will turn to powder on her collarbone and she'll have no chin at all.

She will die of tapioca. Of tassels. Of watching too much space travel.

Here are your choices: *jipijapa* means a Brazilian hummingbird; a hat made from tender young leaves; Hawaiian bread pudding; or—from the Australian colloquial—to be in high spirits following the beginning of study at a college or university.

She asks, Did you feel *jipijapa* when you started college?

So that's your guess?

Not necessarily. I am pausing to ask you a personal question. Were you in high spirits?

I don't remember, I say.

Sure you do, corn nut.

It was twenty years ago. I don't.

Your father got very excited when he went off to school. He wrote gushing letters.

What is your guess, Mother?

You'd have thought that college was a goddamn cathedral.

Time is up.

I love a good bread pudding.

Wrong, I say.

I know, she says. It's the hat of young goddamn leaves. Are you aware that the sluttish postman has not been bringing our mail?

It's not his fault if we don't get written to, I remind her.

He is a slut, though. I've been watching him. He makes house calls on this very block, if you know what I mean.

I really don't, I say.

Please don't act like the virgin you are so bent on remaining.

Anybody with one eye could see what he's up to. Mrs. Poole in the split-level? Mr. Brim in the Oldsmobile? They've been getting their fill of our most venturesome mail carrier.

Who *cares,* I say.

She grunts: It's almost better than television.

On the flickery screen, people in jeans and puffy shirts are learning to waltz. An instructor taps out beats of one-two-three.

I put down the grocery bags and ask, Why are you crying?

I'm not, she says, turning wetly away.

What, do those people all have cancer? Are they dancing to distract themselves?

Isn't it shocking that nobody wants to marry you, with a sunshine attitude like that! Those are just some idiots on public access. I had to switch from my regular channel because (with thumb and forefinger she kneads the loose skin at her throat), because there was an accident.

A crash?

Yes, a crash. The ship crashed. The ship has been lost.

Did the schoolteacher parachute to safety? I ask.

Is this the day your brain decided to stop working? *There are no parachutes in space.* There is cold air and death.

Sorry, I say.

The galaxy is too big out there, my mother says.

The word tonight is *flocculence—*

Don't be coarse, she says.

Your choices are thus: the silence that follows a bad joke; the state of being covered with a soft, woolly substance; the crunch made by teeth on potato chips; the rate of torsion in the flight of seagulls; or an Icelandic sleeping porch built of marble and walrus tusks.

Be nice to have a sleeping porch, she says. You know it's hell on my legs, climbing those stairs every night. Makes them ache to a fare-thee-well. My veins are getting like goddamn garden hoses.

We'll need to install an elevator, I say.

Your dad's insurance won't stretch *that* far.

(It's getting less stretchy all the time.)

You might have to get a job again, sour ball.

I say, Choose or forfeit.

I choose none.

None?

I think they're *all* fake. You've done a trick this time. Whatever I choose will be wrong.

Just choose goddamnit.

I won't, because I don't think it's a real word. I think you made it up—

I ask, Is that your final decision?

She nods. I shut the dictionary. She leans her spoon on the rim of the tapioca bowl, sniffs, tucks her chin. Folds of skin accordion at her neck. James Agee could have described her much better—would have done justice to the weirdness of my mother, her loggishness, her ghouliness, her secret gentleness. He could've spent pages, maybe a whole chapter, doing her justice.

About me, there'd be little to write. *She sits at home of an evening. With mother, with dictionary.* He might have wrung a sentence or two out of my eyes, which are a not-bad shade of blue. He'd have piled adjectives upon this blue, lavished it with taut slippery words until it was unrecognizable as a color and had become—a feeling.

I wonder where the funerals will be, she says.

In the astronauts' hometowns?

Too ordinary.

At the launch pad in Florida?

Too tacky. I'm thinking Arlington Cemetery.

That's for veterans, I say.

And what are they, if not veterans? Soldiers in the space race? Battlers of the galactic elements?

Vomit, I say.

There's that sunshine. There's that charm. Hark!—she cups a hand at the back of her ear—I think I hear the suitors lining up now! Do you hear them? Outside the door? The line is forming *around the block*. Nobody loves a sour ball, sour ball.

James Agee wouldn't have minded; he was sour too. He'd have whispered, We better clean out this mouth of yours! before he kissed it.

Next time I go shopping, I'll be leaving her tapioca off the list. She wants pudding, she can goddamn well figure out how to get it delivered. Or she can put some shoes on for once and hop in the car.

James Agee, please write her into the ground. Tell about the wet earth clumping down onto her coffin. Describe her bone-box with your best, your most precise exaggerations.

In the yellow kitchen, her face is a lump of smile. She has seen the postman getting out of Mr. Brim's car. Dirty deeds, she hoots. Oh, very dirty. She swallows coffee in triumph and I want her to stop smiling, stop watching out the window, stop thinking she *knows*.

Mother, I say.

Daughter?

In case you weren't aware, that rocket ship didn't crash yesterday.

Of course it did, beechnut. I saw it with my own peekers. No survivors.

It crashed in nineteen-*eighty*-something! The teacher has been dead for decades. How can you be so fucking—

Language, she reminds me, and gets up from the table.

Your word tonight is *thole*.

Soul, you say?

Tee-aitch. Here are your choices. To murder someone using brainwaves only; to throw a body into a hole; to sew up a person's face so she can't smile; or to suffer long, to bear, to endure.

What a jolly lineup, my mother says.

I wait. She sips a bite of pudding off the spoon.

I guess I'll pick the most horrible one, then.

Which is?

The long suffer, silly. The endure.

I was a dot in a teenager's egg sac while James Agee was wrecking his looks with smoke and drink and screenwriting. The moment he fell, crumpling on the plastic-taped leather of a taxi seat, I was swinging around in a belly, as yet unfertilized, to sock hop music. He was the man for me and never knew it. He left the planet without being told I was on my way.

My mother has found a new delight to replace her rockets. It is a show about dragons. There is a lot, evidently, to learn about them. They are usually deaf but have excellent eyesight, and it takes a thousand years for a dragon egg to hatch.

She says: I know they aren't real, but maybe they are.

Maybe they are, I agree.

27

Who can tell for certain?

Not us.

Maybe, she says, they only live beneath the remotest mountains. Or in the deepest pockets of the ocean.

From the porch I watch firstlings of heartsease climb the fence. Tiny green shoots fill the pavement cracks and sunned dirt sends its hot smell into my mouth. It's an hour past mail time. Maybe we have gotten none, or my mother was accidentally right and he's been visiting Mrs. Poole on her carpet.

Then he comes whistling round the corner in his gray-blue shorts. He grins at me with a mustached lip. I want to smile back, but I look down instead.

Beautiful day! is his observation.

I want to answer, but my mouth refuses. It makes a little fist on my face.

I bring you treasure, he continues, our jaunty postman, and holds up an envelope from Eternal Meadow Insurance Company. I start to say Thank you, but he is gone before it can come out.

The money won't last forever. I'll have to get a job again. I will work, and my mother will die, and James Agee will live in the pages under my pillow. I carry the check indoors to my mother, who likes to touch money with both hands before it gets deposited. She lifts her eyes from the blue screen, face sweaty and pleased. She has been waiting.

Listen to this, she says. This is marvelous. Dragons have such peculiar diets! The seafaring ones eat starfish only. The ones in caves eat bats and mold. And the meadow-dwellers are thought to survive entirely on honey bees!

Amazing, I say.

Amazing, she agrees.

THE EVERYTHING HATER

My brother has enrolled in a writing class at the community center and says the other students make him want to kill himself and one day soon, he warns us, he probably will. Our mother laughs, but tells me to keep an eye peeled. My duties as the non-suicidal child include frequent phone calls and unannounced visits. I call frequently, and if he doesn't answer I call back until he does. I drive over to his apartment and stay an hour or two, coughing on his smoke, listening to crackly records whose brilliance he says I don't appreciate.

There is often a pile of dishes crusting next to the sink. Not *in* the sink, because Horace needs the sink for watering and draining his large pots of decorative nightshade. You don't have to, he might say feebly, as I turn the taps, to which I reply, It's not a big deal, because it isn't, after all, a big deal to soap and rinse a few cups. So why doesn't he wash them himself? I accuse my mother of raising a boy who can't do his own dishes and of raising a girl who feels obliged to do them. Don't give me that, she says, did you check the bathroom? and I nod and say, Just mouthwash! because it would not ease her mind to tell her what is in my brother's medicine cabinet.

What are you writing about for your class? I ask when the

plates are dripping on the rack, September wind pushing the panes, night ready to fall.

Some bullshit, he says.

Story or poem?

You could call it a story, he says, if you were feeling generous.

About what?

You're asking the wrong question, he says, pressing his finger down on a little spider inching across the stacked guitar cases that serve as a coffee table. Die, die, my darling, he whispers before announcing, A salt-worthy story isn't *about* something—it is that something itself.

Then what is the something that your story is?

Bullshit, my brother replies.

If he happens to be in a good mood, he will ask me a question or two. How is my sell-out job? Have I found a boyfriend yet or is there no man alive under the age of fifty willing to go to bed with me at ten P.M.? Do I derive satisfaction from my sell-out job? Do I remember that I used to be creative, back in childhood when I made dolls out of pebbles and felt? Can I lend him eighty dollars? Does Mom consider him pathetic? Would Dad have considered him pathetic? If eighty's too steep, how about sixty?

When his mood is not good, he goes on choked tirades about the other students in his writing class. Do I understand the ridiculousness of these people? They have experienced *nothing* of life. They are naive, dull-witted, they are sheep blinking in the glint of the blade—which is to say, he explains, they can't think for themselves and have no idea the government's hand hangs poised to slit their chubby throats.

Is that a metaphor? I ask.

No, Horace says.

And the students' writing is so bad—so appallingly, devastatingly bad—the word *wretched* springs to mind and their puny efforts to sound deep fail so miserably the word *failure* is actually charitable and my brother can't figure out why a single one of these people chose to pick up a pen in the first damn place. It's not as if they have talent. It's not as if they have anything, and Horace means *anything*, to say.

Maybe they just like to write, I suggest.

My brother wants to know how you can possibly enjoy doing something at which you suck.

We are nothing for Halloween. In sweatpants, I mix a batch of cookie dough and set the bowl on the couch with two spoons. In sweatpants, Horace comes over with beer, his skull ashtray, and horror movies from Slick Flix where Duke, his sometimes friend, works. He and Duke are speaking at the moment, which means free videos. But the first movie, *Cuddle of Death*, has to be turned off after five minutes because its soundtrack includes a song by a band whose singer used to sing, years ago, in Horace's band. Not only is the song horrendous, my brother says, but can I imagine the agony of listening to caca from the anus of a talentless hack who was once just like Horace (poor and unknown) but now never has to work a day in his life?

Instead of putting in another movie, he opens another beer and starts complaining about his writing teacher. She is too loose with her praise. She says stories are interesting when they're not. It makes these people think they have *potential,* he says. She bats those big yellow eyes and goes, *Interesting*. But it's not! Sex in dorm room: not interesting. White boy traveling in Morocco: not interesting. Old age home: not interesting, *depressing,* unless you make something cool happen, such as mutiny. Patients bludgeoning nurses with walkers, etc.

The bell buzzes. Horace yells, *Après moi,* the razor blades! and I go for the door. Two ghosts and a scary clown hold out plastic pumpkins. I drop a bag of gumdrops into each pumpkin. Thank you, they say without enthusiasm.

You've got boring candy, Horace tells me. Those kids are out there right now talking shit about you.

And my degree of caring about that is . . . ?

Higher than you're willing to let on. You secretly wish you could give them something badass, like miniature guns that shoot chewable bullets. But all you have is piano-teacher candy.

Dad liked gumdrops, I point out.

And you greatly honor his memory by distributing them to pissed children. He had bad taste, face it. He liked bow ties and soft rock. He liked *Mom,* for god's sake! Horace crushes out a dwindled cigarette on the teeth of the skull.

When the beer is gone, cookie-dough bowl licked to gleam, he is still fretting about the singer. It's just *stupid,* he repeats. How did that band get on a *soundtrack?*

It's only *Cuddle of Death*, I reason. It never even came out in theaters.

Yeah, but.

I yawn and he goes to my refrigerator to see if there might be any beer he didn't notice before.

Our parents were the same height—they matched. They traded off reading us bedtime stories, and neither minded reading the same story again and again. Either could fix a fine egg-and-tomato sandwich on short notice. Our mother was better at dancing and driving, and our father had a better sense of humor. Our mother was good at comforting our father when he cried, all those nights when he sat on the couch holding his cheeks, weeping, grunting, shaking his head, and she told us to go to our rooms. Whenever we asked was Dad all right, Mom would say, Sure, goslings, he's just feeling sad today.

After his funeral, we moved from the city to a town so tiny we were able to count its stoplights on two hands. This town is small but not quaint or friendly. The first time Horace got charged with a drunk and disorderly, in front of one of the two local bars, policemen held his face against a brick wall and tapped the back of his head with a flashlight.

We do this a little harder, one cop said, guess what happens to your brains? Smash-o! and the other cop laughed.

Smash-o? Horace repeated afterward, with disdain. What the fuck kind of word is that?

I watched him fiddle with the gauze reddening on his cheek and forehead. It's hard to get bandages to stay fixed on a mouth, so his broken-open lips just went ahead and bled.

Feel like making out? he asked, lurching at me.

Our mother worries first about self-harm and second—a close second—about the fact that Horace refuses to work. Her daughter, at least, has a job, the same job for several years running, even if it's not a very interesting one. Her son hasn't had a job in a year and a half, and she is getting a bit tired, *frankly,* of supplementing the income he makes from selling blood. He sells it as often as they let him, but blood money doesn't go too far. Neither does the cash he gets from being a volunteer for medical tests that turn his feces white. Mom pays most of his bills and I accuse her of gross enabling.

Better to enable than have him move back in with me, she answers. That really took its toll.

She likes us to attend Sunday dinner at her house, because it reminds her of television shows where families eat together on Sundays with gusto and ceremony. Ladling sauced beef onto macaroni, she asks how our respective weeks have gone.

Horace spears a finger of meat and lifts it up for inspection.

I announce, They might put me in charge of planning the new vacation-package campaign.

That's great, goose. To where?

Central Asia.

Horace burbles, An enchanting travel destination, to be sure. All the crime, the heat, and the outdoor plumbing you could ask for! What's your brochure gonna say—*Visit Kyrgyzstan, because it's cheaper than Belgium?*

I, for one, am proud of you, Mom says. It's an exciting opportunity.

If you want exciting, says my brother, you should've seen my class this week. Man, I'm telling you—the action never stops. First we've got a roller-coaster ride of a story entitled "The Final Waltz," the heartwarming saga of a woman who slow dances with her Alzheimer's-ravaged husband. Really innovative material, and so freshly imagined—nary a cliché in sight! Next we're treated to the joy of "Oops I Did It Again and Again," a comical look at twenty-four hours in the life of a teenage slut. How many lacrosse players do you reckon a girl can pleasure in twenty-four hours? Mom, you first.

Horace, *please*.

No, no, come on, give it a go. Two? Five? Ten? Nay, *eleven* this girl manages. The narrator informs us, in no uncertain terms, that such promiscuity is the result of low self-esteem and an absent father. I like a story that spells out its message, don't you? Not quite as subtle as a greeting card, perhaps, but— Fortunately for all, we had our esteemed instructor on hand to lead us in the critique. Know what she said? Know what she told the jellyfish brain who wrote that tale? He slurps another beef slice off his fork. *The way you describe her crouching alone in the janitor's closet, pulling her panties back up, is very moving.*

Maybe it was, I say.

And maybe I am the next Joyce J. Beckett.

Mom asks, What has she said about *your* stories?

Nothing.

Why not?

Because I have turned none in. I haven't been inspired to finish anything. The instructor is not what you'd call inspiring. More like *aspiring*. To be what, I couldn't say. While the rest of us are slowing *expiring* from lack of—

Shall we change the subject? says Mom.

And I forgot to tell you, there's going to be a reading. In, like, early December. The last week of class.

Oh! That's lovely. Are your sister and I invited? Mom's face creaks with the same terrible optimism it did when Horace told her Duke had gotten him a job at the video store. She had no way of knowing my brother would last a total of three days at Slick Flix.

Family and friends, apple juice and cheddar nips, the *works*. The yellow-eyed queen of false encouragement wants us to share our literary bounty with those we love.

On Thanksgiving morning, once the turkey's in, we watch Mom make sweet-potato pie. It was Dad's favorite. He composed a song to sing while it baked: Yammy, yammy, golden yammy, tell me why you taste so yummy. Every Thanksgiving since he died, one of us has sung it instead. It's an embarrassing song and no longer even reminds me of my father. I associate the yams with Horace's amplifier, which exploded the year he tried to accompany my voice with electric guitar. The amp blew out on the first *yummy* and a wire of sparks flew across the air and our mother screamed so hard she began to hyperventilate. Horace stalked off to his room—he was living at home that year—to smoke a bowl, leaving me to get our mother breathing again.

Whose turn is it? Mom asks, sliding the pie onto the rack above the turkey.

I have a sore throat, says Horace.

That must make you a little *hoarse,* I say.

They stare back at me.

Get it? Horace—hoarse—*get* it?

Got it, unfortunately, my brother says.

The night of the first Thanksgiving after we moved to the town of few stoplights, he was pulled over at three in the morning. One cop circled the car, dragging the nose of his gun against its sides, while the other cop prepared a breathalyzer.

Can you, um, not do that? Horace said.

The cop kept walking very slowly around the car. The gun squeaked along the metal. Horace took his mouth off the nozzle and said, You're gonna scratch it!

The cop didn't stop.

Please, my brother said, it was my dad's car.

The cop lifted the gun so it was pointing at Horace. You think your dad wanted you driving drunk in this car?

He wouldn't have minded, declared my brother, as long as I was driving *well.*

Our mother stands still at the sink, hands in apron pockets.

Pie smells good, I say.

What? Oh. . . . She shakes her staring eyes away from the window and says, Where did your brother go?

Upstairs. He said he needed to take a nap.

It's eleven A.M.

Want me to check?

Mom says, I'm just trying to remember what's in my medicine cabinet.

He's got plenty of his own, I want to tell her.

He's a bluffer, I want to say.

Why don't you check, she nods. And I'll baste the carcass.

I knock on the door of the room that was Horace's for the last two years of high school and again after college until our mother kicked him out. Hor, I call. Hor-house! Hello? Are you dead in there?

No reply.

I'm coming in, I say, so cover yourself.

And I open the door.

It's not like the time three years ago, when he got close enough for an ambulance ride (pills). Not like a year ago, when he didn't get close at all (pills again, but too many; he vomited them up). Not like this past summer, when he didn't appear to be trying very hard—knifed his wrists the wrong way and they didn't bleed enough.

All those times it was me who found him, and I prayed so fast my tongue dented the roof of my mouth.

This time I don't pray. I have this hard little thought, a stripe of cold, broken lightning: *Go ahead*.

I have this relief.

It only lasts as long as one breath takes to break in a lung. Then I am yelling, Come on! and hollering, You fucker, come on! I punch the mounded blankets, slamming and slamming my fists into the curled lump of him.

Quit it, Horace says. He wriggles his head out from under the blue knit blanket, and peeks up. Now I'm bruised, he complains.

You're a dick.

It was a *joke*. He picks the orange bottles off the floor and rattles them at me.

I watch him back, quiet, until he can't stand it and looks away. I keep watching. I want my eyes to shoot shame into him, or guilt, or a new conscience that will keep him from ever doing it again. Not the pretending part—the real trying it part. I stare and stare and hope I'm firing beams of living into his brain. Horace wipes a clump of black hair off his face, reaches for his cigarettes on the dresser. Jesus, he says, I'm fine.

It is common for brothers to knife the heads off sisters' dolls, but I didn't know that when I was six. I saw my killed doll and wondered where the blood was. I went sobbing to my father, who was watching his game. Not now, baby, he said, leaning around me to see the screen.

But Horrible committed murder! I shouted.

After the game, my brother was goaded into confessing, and because Dad was in a bad mood—his team had probably lost—he smacked him in the face. Horace, bright-lashed with tears, whispered to me: You will never be forgiven.

Yes I will, I said.

No, you won't.

Yes I will.

Nope.

But please?

Never, Horace said.

Oh *please*? Please please please forgive me?

No matter how much you beg, he said, I will never forgive a tattler.

I report to our mother: He's fine.

Is he? She stirs grated orange peel into a pot of boiling cranberries.

Just taking a little nap.

The boy gets far too much sleep, she says.

The man whose thirtieth birthday is scheduled for the week after Christmas pads downstairs in socks embroidered with little monkeys. A merry noon to ye wenches, he says. Shall I whip up some eggnog?

I hate eggnog.

Then what say you, Mother? Wouldn't you relish a cup of good cheer to inaugurate the holiday season?

She says, I think it would be nice if nobody drank today.

Yeah, that sounds nice. That sounds so *nice!* Have you already dumped out all the liquor? He walks to the sink, peers in, sniffs.

Melodrama, I accuse.

My brother squints at me. I stare back. I won't take my eyes off him. Finally, lightly, he says, You want melodrama, sweetie? Just wait till next Friday. There will be great goddamn truckloads of it to be had.

What's next Friday?

His class reading, Mom reminds me.

Of course she wouldn't forget.

We sit on folding chairs in a sort of rec room with exposed pipes and a troubling reek of foot-vinegar that Horace says is from the yoga classes they hold there. The first reader is a guy with platinum hair and the kind of face I imagine a surfer or wood-cutter would have: red, rubbery, confident. My brother whispers to me, His cock is a worm of flab and he relies on medicine to stiffen it—according to the three women in the class who've slept with him since September.

The second student recites a poem about bathing in poison juice that's gushing from a hole in her arm. After the bath, says the poem, she is finally clean. Revolting glamorizer of drug use, gnashes my brother, that lobotomy-on-legs couldn't write her way out of the plastic bag I'd like to hold over her head until her lungs collapse.

I wonder what he would say about *me* if ever I were to stand at a podium. Tragically boring, he'd explain to whoever was near. She goes to bed early and washes every plate as soon as it's dirty.

There's *nothing* you like, I hiss.

I like you, he points out, and peels a long pink strip of skin away from his thumbnail.

I ask what he's going to read. Our mother, on the other side of Horace, leans to hear his answer.

Nothing, he says.

Mom's face is a punched-in cake.

What do you mean? I say.

I mean nothing, he says. It's not *required by law*.

Then why—

Did we come? finishes Mom in a little screech.

Applause rips forth for the revolting glamorizer. Horace shrugs, fists balled clapless on his thighs. What else have the two of you got to do on a Friday night? he says. Answer me that.

We sit baffled through the rest of the readers. At long last the instructor takes the podium to thank everyone for coming and to say what a great group of writers this has been to work with.

Lies, Horace whispers.

She's pretty, I notice.

He scowls.

She's *really* pretty.

If you like that type.

What type?

The pretty-enough-to-know-it-and-be-arrogant-about-it type. And beauty doesn't do her much good if she's a fool. That is, if her taste in literature is about as refined as a wrecking ball.

That is, if she tells that blond moron his shit is compelling when it certainfuckingly is *not*. Can she be that dumb? Maybe she just wants a taste of his wilted—

I'll wait for you outside, Mom says in a tiny voice.

Horace stares at the podium where the instructor, surrounded by students, is laughing and nodding. Around one finger she twists a strand of shimmery dark hair. My brother watches her, frowning, jaw clenched. He slaps at his jacket for cigarettes, still watching.

I breathe through my mouth against the foot-vinegar. Ready, Hor?

Yeah, he says, motionless.

The instructor starts making her way in our direction. Handshakes and smiles slow her progress. I hear a strangled hum from my brother's throat—an attempt to clear itself.

Leaving already? she cries upon reaching us.

Horace shrugs. I wait in vain to be introduced.

I can't believe you didn't read, she says, why didn't you *read?* and she hits him on the shoulder. She is even younger-looking up close.

He shrugs again.

Some of us are going out, she says. You should come. If you won't read, at least you can drink.

I wait for him to pony up some sarcastic little phrase, but he and his mouth are motionless.

Okay, well. The instructor reaches up with an elastic band to rein in her splendid hair.

I think she was flirting with you, I remark in the car.

Mom snaps to attention. Flirting? Who?

Don't be absurd, Horace says.

At the next Sunday dinner, as we're gamely swallowing our

mother's stab at West African peanut stew, Horace looks even more depressed than usual. I watch Mom's glance skitter to his ashy, swollen-eyed face, then dart away before he can yell, You're wearing a *look of pity*.

Goo, she says, what's bothering you?

He shrugs. I never got to workshop my story. I had it finished by the last class, but there wasn't time. We had to discuss the tale of a girl and her horse and then some sci-fi crap.

You can sign up for another workshop, can't you? Do they offer a winter session? I'd be happy to cover the cost of a second one, if you—

Yeah, well, *maybe*. I have to check who's teaching.

There's a smear of peanut sauce on his chin. Mom reaches to wipe it with her napkin, and I get tears of disgust at the back of my mouth.

It is too cold to roll down the window even a little, so his cigarette takes over the car. Why do I always let him smoke?

Can you put that out, it's getting gross in here.

Almost done, he says.

No, will you throw it out *now*? I can't breathe.

Tobacco does not grow on trees.

This is *my* car.

Well, good for you. He takes a last, long, sumptuous drag, cracks the window, and tosses the butt. Here's one. What does God use to clean his teeth? Wait for it—*transcendental floss!* He checks to see if I'm smiling. He clears his throat, says, So what do you want for Christmas?

I don't know.

Come on.

Haven't thought about it.

Oh. He gnaws his thumb. Something wrong?

No.

Oh.

We are in front of his apartment building. I rub my fore-head with two fingers. He tugs the orange scarf tighter at his mother-wiped chin. When you think of what you want, let me know, he says. Unless it costs a lot.

Good night, I say.

I don't phone or visit my brother for a week. Every day after work I drive straight home.

My mother calls to ask if I'd like to come over and decorate the tree. I got a very shapely one this year, she says.

I tell her sure. And has she checked if Horace wants to join us? I could pick him up on my way over—

No need, she flutters, he's already here. He just put on the angel.

Oh, I say, and don't feel like going anymore.

It is dark but not late; people are in their houses, cooking, changing out of work clothes, settling in. Horace's windows are ablaze so I park the car. Gather the takeout cartons. That you? he croaks through the intercom.

It's me.

Jesus Christ, he says.

The floor is ankle-deep in records and beer cans. He squats in front of the stereo, adjusting knobs. He's drunk, I gather, from the slowness of his mouth, the droop of his red lids. He says, You can be here, but be quiet.

What are you doing?

Making a mix.

Want some food? I went to Poblano Palace—

Feh, he says.

I get one plate, one fork, one square of paper towel from the kitchen. I pour one glass of water. With my dinner spread out on the guitar case, I eat and listen to Horace choose songs. He keeps shaking his head, rewinding. He writes each title carefully on the back of an envelope.

This is a fucking great tune, he remarks over his shoulder. Don't you think? Shit, it's great.

I chomp rice and guacamole.

And the one before, too. In fact this whole mix is great. I would go so far as to say killer? Alas, no ears shall appreciate.

Who's it for?

For someone who will not afuckingppreciate. Hencefore I am not going to give it. But it's for her anyway.

Who?

Her. The unappreciator. Where are my coffin nails?

By your foot. So who is it, Hor? (Although I am pretty sure that I know.)

None of your bitchwax. He lights a cigarette and clutches his knees to his chest. I can't believe how good this mix is.

Why won't you give it to her?

One, she wouldn't like it. Two, she'd think I'm creepy for making it. Three, I have no way of finding her. Who knows where she roams? She might be here, she might be there, she might be in my underwear. He giggles, eyes closed.

Have you looked in the phone book?

And the point of that would be *what,* exactly? Do you believe—he swigs from a can, notices it is empty, picks up the one next to it—that many a girl dreams of consorting with an elderly shut-in who is doing with his life, hmm, let's see, *not a thing?* And who can't, because he has no car or for that matter valid driver's license, take her to the movies?

A girl might like him anyway, I say.

Why?

I could answer *because he's handsome,* or *because he's smart,* or *because he'd serenade her sweetly on the guitar.* But other people are wiping his chin on too regular a basis. He lets it get dirty, knowing there's a napkin on the way.

I haven't yet told my mother that in the new year my eye will not be so peeled. She will say, But he has such trouble taking care of himself!

And I will say, It wasn't your fault about Dad.

Their Christmas lists are brief: money or what can be traded in for money (brother) and a good cookbook (mother).

You must want more than a cookbook, I prod.

No, I've got everything I need, she answers, clamping one hand on my shoulder, the other on Horace's. Have a good expedition! and she pulls the orange scarf snugger around his neck.

We walk in the glittery cold to the center of town, where ribbons festoon the street lamps and plowed snow hardens on the curbs. You haven't told me what you want, he complains, and there's only two days until Jesus.

Surprise me.

It'll have to be an economic surprise.

At the fire station, we stop to admire the trees. They are selling some really tall ones. How come Mom bought such a fucking midget? he says. These ones are killer. She should've gotten one here.

Can you say one positive thing ever?

I say many positive things.

Um, not really.

Half an hour ago I told you I liked your new peacoat, *did I not?* Where are we headed? I'm fucking cold. That is—I am delightfully cold. Cheerfully chilled. Felicitously freezing. See? *Positive*.

Let's finish Main Street then get some lunch.

Only two days left, he repeats with fake gloom. He'll be as relieved as I will to have Christmas over with. I never miss my father more than on the Eve, when he used to read us "'Twas the Night Before Christmas" and make up little extra parts where the reindeer said things.

I know Mom told us cookbook, Horace continues, but I think we should get her a dating guide for seniors. *To those about to die, we salute you and your waning libidos. . . .* He takes my mittened hand, settles it in the crook of his elbow, and adjusts his lope to my shorter strides. Linked, we cross the snow-scabbed bridge and follow the curve of Main Street toward the outdoor mall, directly across from the bar where cops pushed my brother's face against a brick wall until the blood trickled onto his sneaker laces. Horace still drinks at this bar. He is becoming one of those town guys who sit on a stool, watch the game, flirt with the bartender, and at last call leave alone.

Go on in, he says, lifting his cigarette, I want to finish this.

A rope of bells chimes. The bookstore is warm and quiet. The woman behind the counter, bent over a book, says without looking up: Help you find anything?

Oh shit, I say.

It is Horace's writing instructor.

She looks up.

I need something for my brother, I say.

What does he like to read?

Everything. Except, you know, crap.

She nods, twisting a piece of hair around her finger.

He's a writer himself, I add, so he's kind of critical.

Will she say, Actually I'm a writer too! and will I ask if she ever teaches and will she say, Yes, at the community center! and will I mention Horace and try to tell, from how her eyes move, what she thinks of him?

No. She gets up and leads me to a table display. Here are some new titles he probably won't have seen yet.

She returns to her stool and I pretend to scrutinize dust jackets. Sweat seeps down my ribs. Through the snowflake-painted window I watch the back of Horace's head. *Her—the unappreciator—who knows where she roams?* And him, the hater, who roams in a tiny circle from his apartment to the blood bank to the bar and back again.

I could leave right now, before he sees her. Take his arm and hop away, drag him until he starts running, gets ahead of me, glances over his shoulder to chide, Come on! I could chase after him laughing and he would laugh too and my nose would run and we'd stagger on the snow, shouting, until we were long past the mall and the bar and the brick where a splash of his blood can still be detected if you look close.

Him and me, no one else.

Back at the counter I say, Nothing caught my eye.

The instructor nods and the bell-rope clatters behind me. I see her see him. I hear him stop in his tracks. She smiles; her black lashes flitter. She says, *That* wouldn't happen to be your brother, would it?

Yeah, I say, turning. Horace stands pressed against the door. His face has gone a lunar white.

Hello stranger, calls the instructor.

Oh, he says.

My mouth is ready with all kinds of sabotage. *We have to be getting back. We're late for our movie. We're meeting our mother for lunch. Horace, didn't you need to stop by the hardware store?*

How've you been? the instructor asks.

Keeping my head out of the oven, Horace replies, and cackles with unusual vigor. Incredibly, she laughs too. More of a bark, really. Together they laugh a lot longer than the remark warranted. My brother comes to lean against the counter. He smells like smoke and toothpaste.

You know, I wanted to tell you, she says, since we never got a chance to discuss your story in class. . . .

He bends closer.

I make for the door and keep a careful hold on the bells as I open it, though god knows what for—Horace wouldn't notice my leaving if I screamed the whole way out. A swift glance back through the snowflakes: she is laughing again. Perhaps he's talking shit about the impotent woodcutter, or regaling her with a hilarious account of finding, when he came home from tenth grade, our father asphyxiated in his car: *It gave a whole new meaning to the phrase "blue in the face"!*

Her barking can be heard through the glass and clear across the parking lot as I walk—reminding myself to root for him— back up Main Street in the direction of home.

HEART SOCKETS

On a rain-black morning she inches up and asks me to do some
groundwork. Cut through the glass mask the new boy wears.
Drop her name at his feet, please, and see what he picks up.
Struck speechless herself whenever he's near, she wants me to be
the talker. I am so much older, she thinks, I won't be after him
myself. I have no desires left, she probably thinks.

You just need to do the groundwork, the girl explains.
Once that's laid, I step in.

The supervisor stops pacing, lets his crotch hover at my shoulder, and waits. I give him my heart and he pinches it between
thumb and pinky, testing. We are told to make hearts firm and
flesh them strong, stitch them tight in the glare of our room, tall
and white, with long wood tables and plates of silver instruments.

Garbage! says the supervisor.

But the stitches are good, I say.

No keeping, he says, it's shit. He turns and brays to the
room, We are not in the jack o' lantern business here!—his
skull shining globy in the white, chilly light. Tidy stitches! he
howls. Tidy, tidy!

With his barks and warbles, he ruins the room. I, cowering,

tell my ears don't listen. My stitches stagger, wrung clumsy. There are so many hours before the day can end.

The animals wait at home, splinted and bandaged. Codling, elver, owlet, smolt. Human milk works on these wild babies. Even the eel? Especially the eel. It finds the breast quickly. My nipple is bigger than its head but it licks drops. The young owl's beak is nimble; the codling's lips are a wet pleasure. The infant salmon sucks longer than a human child can. Hurt young animals heal quicker than you think. Some rest, some milky drink, some affection is a marvelous cure. Behind my house are shelves for them, tin-roofed, padded with straw. Clean troughs for the fish. Old soft shreds of clothes that don't fit me anymore, which the babies nose and trod to make little beds.

Across the gravel lawn from the sewing room is a shackish building they say was once used as a buttery. What happens in a buttery other than butter? A milkmaid with skirts foaming at her plump neck getting pounded by the assistant gamekeeper? The company uses it for coffee and small food you can buy on your break. From tucked against the window I watch the new boy watch his own feet dig in the gravel. He doesn't come inside. He stands scratching the ground with a toe, walks from one fence to the other, runs waving through a grist of bees outside the buttery door. I pray they won't sting but his skin looks easy to bite. His skin looks like a newborn cougar's pelt. He is dash, with damp curls, a pinstriped suit, a sharkskin belt. I don't know him more than a face through fogged windows when I sit with my cup waiting to work again, but I have noticed he wears the same pinstripes every day. His face blown perfect like blue glass animals that cost a thousand dollars make my fingers throb to build a new and better than anything heart. His face looks like good work.

I watch the dash boy dance for minutes on end. He stops when he sees nobody is watching. (He can't know I am, from the brown window.) Done dancing, he takes off one shoe and hurls and the shoe flies where I can't see it. Break is done and time to work but I take the long way around the back of the buttery. In the low-grown bride's-breath hemming the wall lies his shoe. The shoe is, I notice, a creeper. It is purple and furry and, like any creeper, arrow-toed; it's a fashion you don't see much anymore. I see it and am glad. It means first I have an excuse for talk, a question to ask him—*why did you throw a shoe into flowers?*—and second that the boy knows old, good styles. Third it means he is a little trickster maybe. Nobody else in this no-talking place would raise an eyebrow long enough to play a game with shoes. The other workers are dead with their eyes open.

Last night the wolf pup coughed up his own swallowed teeth. Kept brushing the floor with his snout, as if nervous or hunting, then coughed and coughed and spat the teeth into a little pile, shiny with stomach-juice. I washed the teeth and dried them. Now they sit, a row of yellow three, on the sill above the kitchen sink.

The creeper sits under my jacket all afternoon. It stinks bright and I hope nobody thinks it is my body. The new boy, one-shoed, is at a table by the wall. He is making, I notice, scanty progress on his red handful of silk and stuffing—keeps lifting his head to look around, opening his mouth to talk. They won't talk back! But, like me, he tries. He starts to sing. He whispers, chirrs, and hums. He recounts the plot of a sad movie that came out before he was born.

Necessary? hollers the supervisor. Your loud voice? Is it?

It's too quiet in here, says the boy.

And it might get even quieter, says the supervisor, once I run my thickest strung needle through your lips and *pull*.

Here are my questions:

Why do your eyes remind me of canoes?

Who bought you that pretty suit that fits you pretty badly?

What last thing did you think of last night before sleep? Mine was black stars lashed to the bottoms of canoes.

Have you ever stayed alone in your room for more than one day at a time playing nurse with wound?

In the gravel, after our shift, I hand over the creeper. The boy smiles and tucks it toe-first into his back pocket. I hate it, he says—meaning *here,* I know, because so do I.

I miss it bad, he confesses.

Miss what?

The stem. The grit. The white.

Pardon? I say.

Those mean road. Old terms.

He is young, so he heard them on the radio. He read them in a book. I say, You miss the road?

Bad.

When were you on it?

In childhood, he says.

He is just like the babies on shelves behind my house, except his limbs and fins aren't broken and he can feed himself. But the youngness—the wetness—the way he's eager. His mouth I wouldn't dive a needle into; I would gently guide it to my milk. He would suck until he didn't want more. His lips would be softer than a codling's.

You're that person, he says, that lives in the scary zoo?

I live in a house, I say, not far from town.

But it's a *scary* one, right, it's a spook den, the kind of place nobody goes alone?

I go there alone, I correct him. And my animals are there. I rescue hurt ones.

But you yourself, insists the boy, must be a little off the beaten brain-path.

He has heard people talking about my cages and troughs, my babies barking the whole day and crying the whole night. He thinks something's not firing all the way upstairs in me.

This is a job, he declares, only vegetables or work-release people take. He gets the shoe from his pocket, steers his foot in.

I ask what, if so, brings *him* here.

Investigative journalism, he clucks. I'm deep undercover. Does the supervisor whip or burn you?

No, he's just cranky, I say, to play along with this fatigued joke. I am humoring him. I am dry and old and hot for him. Under my jacket the nipples stand stiff, want sucking. What are you here for? I ask again.

I'm a vegetable too! he says.

(You are a newborn, slick with birth canal.)

Just kidding, he says. I'm a hitchhiker.

(You crack yourself up, you faker imp, you are nothing but a wet thing, velvet mouth!)

I'm actually a tailor's apprentice, he says, who's learning to sew.

(You're a mouth where I fit.)

I am jealous of whatever bodies have fallen under him before today, opened for his skin, whatever other bodies wetter than my old hot hurting one. It's like seeing from the street a Saturday night family in its window, bent at table, the mother and father and child—that same envy. I have a talented mind for matching one feeling to another. A caught scarf on the bus seatback, for instance, is the hand on your neck of someone who knows you but when you turn around, nobody's there.

It was the only job I could find this summer, admits the boy, and this answer sounds truer, but I don't trust him whole. He is barely out of his mother's clutch. Some of us here are old, even if we're not. We get old from keeping out of the way of things.

Elephant seal milk is fat-clogged so rich that a pup gains nine pounds a day. Because she doesn't eat while nursing, a mother seal sheds five hundred pounds in a month of milk.

The forgotten assignment burns back into my mouth. *Mention the girl.* But what is her damn name? I can barely remember her face but oh, I know it's smooth, it matches the boy's, soft as a furred fruit skin. Their cheeks pressed together would be too much soft to bear. The girl has been at the job only a month or two. She drifted in just as she'll drift, not long from now, back out. While she's here, she wants distraction. She wants love gathered on her behalf, the boy drawn by sly strokes into her nearness where, stunned by her charms, he will gape and kneel down. She hasn't yet asked me to write a poem for her to memorize, but I won't be shocked if she does. Her name? It might as well be Calf, since Calf is more fitting than any Jen or Stephanie, really far more accurate.

Here are my questions:

If you saw a hundred-legger run down your wallpaper at night, churning every leg, scratching and whispering, would you kill it with the sole of your creeper? Or would you even be afraid?

Do your lungs ever clot with worry on the weekends?

Does your brain bleed nails of ideas you think are so good until you say them to someone else and the person's face shows you how bad the ideas are?

Does the skin on your feet shiver the second before you step into a bath? Does the hair stand up on your belly?

Calf plows into me on my way up the steps. Drool flecks the splits in her lips, a little girl's drool, saliva of a sparkle and clarity that mean she's not yet acquainted with the cloudier waters of wanting. She whispers, Saw you talking yesterday after work. What did he say? What were the *exact words?*

We didn't get far, I tell her.

But you were talking for at least five minutes, she accuses.

About weather.

Did you get information? Girlfriend? Wife?

He's a bit short in the tooth for marriage, I remind her.

At break, the boy catches up to me on the gravel, says, Your house is a dead hard mark.

First what does that mean, and second how would you know?

A place, he says, only approachable by an expert tramp. I saw it last night from the road.

I say, That must have been a very informative hobo textbook.

Book? he says. What?

Why were you watching my house from the road?

I just wanted to see what it would look like.

I am old enough to be your much older sister, I decide to tell him.

So? he says.

So, I say.

So it's not like I'm affected by that information! and his moist mouth curls angrily. Old vegetable person, he adds.

Slippy eel runt! I hiss.

Maker, he shouts, of no sense!

But his blue glass animal face makes me want to build a heart so much better than the crap we throw together at work, those red synthetic pillows to decorate the beds of hospital children, for pets to ruin with chewing, for dull men to disappoint women with on anniversaries.

Here are my questions:

What do you eat for breakfast? Do you eat breakfast at all or do you play the game of lurker on the grit-stem-white and go hungry for whole hours after waking? *Coffee only and black because no cream is tougher but some sugar please because my mouth wants it.*

What is in your pinstriped pocket? I will guess a small mirror, a dollar, a matchbook from the one fine restaurant you've ever been to, a map of the road that runs past my house.

If you found me in the woods, strewn flat across a pinecone path, would you hold the mirror at my mouth to see if my breath whitened the glass?

Calf corners me at day's end, as we file out, time for home. Takes my balled hand, pries it open for a small book wrapped in blue sugar paper. Give him this, she says.

You give it, I say, pushing the book back to her.

You! she says, shriek-soft.

But why?

It's anonymous, Calf explains.

What if he thinks it's from me?

She honks a sun-drenched laugh, says, I'm not worried.

Is it poetry? I ask.

Her shoulders scrunch at her unroped golden neck. It's amorous reflections, she says.

It takes me twelve seconds to read the book. Only four of its pages have been written on. *Do you ever feel,* says the first in black flowered script, *like a house with no walls?* The next page says, *I do!* On the third page: *Lovers are walls for each other. Do you ever feel like you want some shelter? I will be it for you.* On the last page: *Who do you think is the prettiest girl at our work? Figure out who, and that will be the person who wrote this.*

I doubt Calf meant for this cheap-bound love letter to be philosophical, but innocently she has made it so. She is a confident little cow. I put the book in the bucket I use for scrapings from the animals' shelves. As I go about my evening chores, feeding and cleaning, the blue sinks deeper under the brown.

Day after day of no reaction from the boy—he's his usual moping, pinstriped self—and the girl gets weepy. *Has he picked another?* she is wondering under her sniffles.

The supervisor chastises her twice in one morning for sloppy seams. These guys face a life of wear and tear! he shouts to the room, lifting Calf's heart in the air as a lesson. If a joint splits, they're done for! Your job is to make sure the mothereffing seams are tough as teeth.

The polliwog has a cut foot. A smashed bottle half-sunk in the river mud made a slice in the webbed flesh. When it's a grown frog, its hop will be shaky, but it will hop.

Day after day and Calf gets fed up, as I knew she would. Boredom has killed her shyness and she's ready, though shuddering, to seek him out. It happens in the yard. The boy has been standing alone, as is his custom, when she walks up and crosses her arms and frowns at the gravel. He takes up her downcast, tongue-tied slack (I see through the buttery window) and makes what must be a joke, from how she laughs and lets her lashes do their work.

They make a soft-skinned pair. I hear them gurgling and chortling. Their laughs run through the open buttery door, falling to rest at our old feet while the cups of coffee cool, as we wait to go back to our needles.

When you cuddle an owlet in your palm, it sobs so quietly you think the sound is feathers rustling. Bend close, and you can tell it's noise from a tiny throat.

When you nurse a baby eel, don't leave its mouth at your nipple too long. It won't know when to stop licking. Elvers can drink so much milk it floods their finger bodies, drowns the organs, bloats and swells them to death. I don't let that happen anymore. I am strict with milk time.

I would like to forget those two faces getting close to each other, closer now and closest, which is kissing, which I didn't see them do but know they're doing away from our work, hidden stripped to skin in the carpet-walled basement of his parents' house. Or her parents' house. They both have parents still, parents to pet them, to feed them in the morning and before bed.

A forgetter's heart is better built here, in my own yard, than in the dread stillness of the stalled white room whose windows give onto a gravel sea. I assemble my materials. Molted snake skin for the muscle-bag, gosling feathers to stuff it, shed smolt scales to protect it from puncture. For thread, the blood-stiff twine I used to suture the polliwog's foot. For mast, a shard of wood from the splint on the hedgehog's cracked leg. For crowning touch, fastened with glue, the wolf pup's fangs from the windowsill.

I'll make it in my yard, under the sun, against the boy who's run off into the white with a pack slung across his flimsy shoulders. The straps will chafe that cougar pelt. And does Calf lumber feckless behind, her own pack hung jangly around her neck?

Listen, he tells her, skidding his grimy thumb down a page of the train-hopper's manual, it says *devil-may-care*. I think we're supposed to look more devil-may-care.

My handiwork is finished by evening. The baby salmon blink up from the troughs and the turtles venture tiny wrinkled heads to see my face smiling down—See what I did today? as I dangle the heart in a flashlight beam, the best one ever stitched.

I am leaking heavy onto my shirt, two sopping moons, the mild night a cold sleeve between wet skin and milk-drenched cotton. And the turtles, the fish, the gosling, the owlet whose torn wing is near healed and soon to be flown on again hear my voice and understand that I am happy with what I've made. Unlike the napkin of muscle beating wetly in my chest, this heart will catch. And it will burn.

HOW HE WAS A WICKED SON

After some weeks in the hospital, I went to a nursing home for the young. One winter afternoon I was delivered to its lounge, empty except for a big-bellied kid reading a gun catalog and a hippie slouched on a chair doing what appeared to be nothing. Beds of fluorescent lights whirred above. Fish tanks gurgled on either side of a large television.

The pudgy kid looked up, blinked, snorted, and said, Did somebody get lost on the way to the death-pop concert?

The hippie laughed.

I looked around for people in charge, and saw none. The hospital van driver dropped my duffel bag on the carpet and said, Enjoy your stay, son.

It was a yellow-brick bungalow moated by a balding lawn on a cul-de-sac in St. Paul, Minnesota. The children of the cul-de-sac rode past on their bikes yelling *Eyesore of neighborhood that once was respectable!* but they didn't ride too close. They had been warned. If a soccer ball sailed from their game to land on our lawn, it stayed there until one of us threw it back into the street—or kept it, more often the case, to slam against walls and light on fire.

It wasn't a place you were happy to be, but I liked its routines.

Food cooked by other people. Soap in the bathroom. Sheets washed twice weekly. And there was a boy named Julian I couldn't stop looking at; when he came home at night from his job at the candle factory, I considered myself lucky to live there.

We all gathered in the lounge on Sunday and Tuesday evenings to express concerns, confess to misbehaviors, hoot and holler. People complained about the undercooked chicken or the injustice of being grounded for not making your bed. I kept quiet during these meetings, scrunched against the wall by the bubbler with Ginna, who whispered assessments of our peers. No knowledge of ass from elbow, she said of Jerome. Legs wide two-four-seven, of Graciela. Medically impotent, of Arnold. Nice but terrible haircut, of Vincent. Thinks he is God's gift, of Julian.

In the mornings we stood in the meds line, which swam with sour breath. People craned to see what everyone else was getting—who might be on antipsychotics, or herpes medication, or extra-high dosages.

Shit they're giving me makes my dick soft, said Jerome.

All of them do, said Arnold, except the ones that just stop you from coming.

I don't have those side effects, declared Vincent. It takes a lot more than that to stop my johnson. But what does it do to girls?

We looked at Ginna, who scowled.

Probably just makes them dry, said Arnold.

I take vitamins, I announced. I don't have mental health issues.

That sent them howling. Oh, no sir, I don't have no *mental health issues,* shrieked Jerome. I'm just visiting here for a fucking vacation.

Keep it down, yelled the tech. This is not *Romper Room.*

Vincent tugged on the lapel of my velour blouse. Timothy, why you always dressing for funerals?

Ginna explained, Because black is how he feels on the—

But the *makeup*? You're not a chick!

I said nothing, reminding myself that Vincent had the hair of a tiger handler in the Canadian circus and was wearing a shirt that said *Gone Crazy, Back Soon.*

When it was my turn in line, the tech handed over a paper cup of B-12s and asked wearily how it was going.

Great, I said.

No, I mean, *really.*

It's going really great.

Are you working out your problems with Chuckie?

Oh yes, uh huh!

His stubby fist under my chin: *You touch me, I beat you senseless.* He had petitioned for a room change, which they denied, telling him it was a good opportunity to practice tolerance. *But don't get any ideas, you fucking little fruit.* He kept the lights on at night to prevent me from sneaking over to fondle his balls.

We smoked on the porch, which was always cold. Wind gusted off the great plains to churn in frozen tiding against its rails. Every day after breakfast I huddled there, cupping my cigarette with the other unemployed people. The house rule was you had to get a full-time job. Not just any job would do. You couldn't be a stripper or bartender or even a waiter, nothing that bore resemblance to the old lives we had led. People were encouraged to apply at sporting-goods stores or car washes.

Johnnycake, a cook by trade, had been there two months without lifting a finger. He weaseled around the rule with complaints about his crippling hep C fatigue. The deeper reason, he told us, was pride. I cannot work beneath my calling! he said. I been in the weeds at some of the world's finest restaurants. What I'm gonna do, the golden arches fry station? *Please, motherfucker.*

You're just a lazy bitch, said Arnold.

Would you like to see my chart? It's the medical history of a dead man. I should be *underground,* boy, but I happen to be alive. For how much longer, no one can predict. Look into my eyes. See the jaundice?

I don't see shit, shrugged Arnold, who didn't have a job either and had been there longer than Johnnycake. He had bleeding green tattoos and a scragglish mustache that usually held a crumb or two. When he looked at me, which wasn't often, I felt the contempt like a dull radar beam. I feared he had sized me up accurately. *Spoiled brat, what do you know about suffering?*

Ginna was my only friend. We sat in the cafeteria mostly. I watched her devour the cookies, lemon bars, potato chips, and plates of iced cake that were set out each night after dinner to appease us until next morning's cereal. She was, she explained, eating her way into oblivion. It's the only crime left, she said, so fuck it. Each week I noticed her getting a tiny bit thicker. She could no longer wear the vinyl pants or black plastic camisoles she had brought from Detroit.

One afternoon we drove to the mall and picked out sweatpants, lumberjack shirts, a huge puffy ski vest in metallic silver. Ginna bought me a candle in a jar laminated with the Virgin Mary. When the bags were in the car she said, Can we just drive?

Dinner was not for another hour; there was space, time to kill. We drove. I loved my car for putting us in motion. White-furrowed streets, big iron sky. In motion, there was nothing to worry about. There was dance music on the radio and Ginna's cigarette perched out the window and the heater baking our faces.

My hatchback, cerulean with oyster interiors, had stuck with me loyally through recent bad times. I had never lent it to the men I owed money. Never wrapped it around any poles or bridge abutments. Never traded it for a week's worth of magic beans. After I left the hospital, my father agreed to drive it out along the cheese roads from Eau Claire. Excuse for a visit, he said briskly. I was gladder to see the car than him. He bought me a massive steak dinner at the St. Paul Hotel and we were both on our best behavior.

You do whatever they tell you, he kept saying. Whatever the hell the problem is, I want it cured.

Okay Dad, I said, because he had brought the car. And pulled lawyerly strings to get my felony charge dropped. And paid the very large hospital bill. I prayed hard for God to make me grateful.

What're you doing? asked my father uneasily. I opened my eyes; he took another swallow of gin.

Let's skip dinner, I told Ginna. Keep driving. All these lakes around here, we can find one, walk across it.

She yawned. No, honey, I'm not getting grounded at this stage of the game. I have endured fourteen weeks of that place. I'm on the home stretch. You'll know what I mean in a couple of months.

But please?

And you have your own interests to protect. If they kick you out, there'll be no more loverboy. No more Julian of the craggy cliffs. No more Julian I hardly knew ye but I did so want to suck thee off. Julian who never speaks to—

He does too! Yesterday he was coming out of the laundry

room and I was on the phone with my dad and he looked at me and smiled and said *Hey* in a shy voice.

Sucker, said Ginna.

Yes, I was—for swollen lips, gloomy stare, scrawny hips, hacked-off hair. You know those advertising campaigns where you're supposed to wonder if the models are really models or just accidentally well-made people they picked off the street, kids whose scars and freckles are not painted on, who seem too intelligent to shop at the store being advertised and thereby convince you that the clothes they're wearing are worth the price? Julian looked like those ads. His perfect cheekbones were humbled by a smear of pimples around the mouth. He wore damp cardigans prickly with strands of hair flecked orange from last year's dye jobs. I wanted to jump into his malnourished arms. I wanted him to dream about putting his head on my shoulder. I wanted him to tell me the names of his favorite books, and play me albums on the turntable he had prized enough not to pawn.

In the meantime, I launched tiny smiles from across rooms.

On a morning of unbelievable good fortune he stood with us—the destinationless—on the smoking porch, wrapped in a red wool scarf, and announced that they were hiring at the place he worked.

Where's that, Little Professor? said Johnnycake.

The candle factory, said Julian. It's completely mindless. Eight an hour.

Why ain't you there?

Took a personal day. He mouthed to me, *I'm going record shopping.* I stared back, anchoring my bottom lip against the gape of shock, flicking ash onto my shoes. Was this pretty-mouthed, green-eyed creature really talking to me? Before he even got the words out (*Want to ride along?*) I was saying yes.

He said, You have a vehicle, do you not?

Yes!

I'll drive, he said. If that's okay.

My father's instructions, upon delivering the car, had been: *Do not let a single one of those criminals lay a hand on the steering wheel.* The hatchback was just three years old. The one thing on this earth registered in my own name.

I've been here longer, reasoned Julian. I know the roads. You're fresh from the hospital.

I got here a month ago, I said.

His gorgeous brows went up. That long? Shit. Time travels at unusual speeds.

On the sign-out clipboard in the office, I wrote *Job Hunt* next to my name. The tech called after me, Try Hot Topics at the Mall of America. The kids who shop there dress like you. You could recommend your favorite brand of eyeliner.

Julian wrenched back the driver's seat to make room for his legs. He fingered the picture of Jesus dangling from the rearview and asked, Is this supposed to be ironic?

I guess, I said.

Whatever *floats.* So where'd you go to college?

Um, Yale? I said.

Oh really? I was at Harvard for a brief while, myself.

I tried to think of where Yale was. Somewhere in Massachusetts.

I studied semiotics, continued Julian. The postmodern condition. God died first, then all the authors. He waited for me to nod, so I did. It was hard to concentrate with his corduroyed thigh so close, wiry muscle straining the fabric. His thigh. His *groin.*

Were you a banger? he asked.

No, just pills.

*Encapsul*ated! He lit a cigarette. Consider yourself lucky. Hypodermic love affairs are hard to shake. Can I smoke in this car?

You can do whatever you want.

I like that system. He reached over to tweak my earlobe. It was not a brotherly gesture. My face flooded like a great bloody plain. I hadn't kissed anyone since my days of paddling on dance floors in chemical surf. What if I couldn't remember how? What if the hard little scab on Julian's lip got snagged in my molars?

But there was no kiss. He took his hand back and put it on the radio dial. No stations in this cow town. How do people *live* here? Don't you think it's incredible?

That they listen to bad radio?

— No, he said, I mean the grim and gaudy spectacle of the postindustrial Grain Belt. The subaltern longing.

Yes, I said cautiously.

We rolled into the parking lot of Caribou Coffee. The engine idled and Julian turned to me, switching on a blast of bottle-green eyes. Could you spot me some cash for a drink? I haven't gotten paid yet this week. And my parents have been detaching with love.

It would be my pleasure.

Thanks, sweetie.

Sweetie sounded clunky in his mouth, but I wasn't complaining. I would take the crumbs. I would saunter proudly into Caribou with this fine creature on my arm, or next to my arm. The coffee shop was staffed entirely, except for the manager, by residents of our house. They greeted us with hollow enthusiasm, angry that we weren't at work ourselves.

When you gonna get gainfully employed, man? demanded Jerome. They'll kick you out soon.

Let them do as they may, I said.

Julian was on the other side of the espresso machine talking to Anne Sarah. I didn't much like Anne Sarah; she had two names, which smelled of ambition. She was pursing her lips at my Julian. She was throwing her hair and she had plenty to throw, huge glossy locks that had needed at least a half-gallon of bleach. She put a blue straw between her teeth and let it dangle. I thought I heard him say, What time do you get off? but this was not possible, since how could the phrase of a frat boy, a common hustler, come out of Julian's elegant mouth? Anne Sarah said something too low for me to catch. She was by now *sucking* on the straw, hoisting it slowly up and down.

Jerome rang up my tea and a large coffee. Both were cold by the time Julian finished his conversation with the straw-wielder.

Sorry sweetie, he said, we were talking about God.

Ginna, my ethical thermometer, gave stern counsel. He's already sweating two of my roommates—your chances are slim. You need to abandon this pipe dream.

Blah, I said merrily. How are you defining *sweating*?

Dragging under the stairs by the cafeteria. Attempting to fornicate with.

That's a lie!

Why would I lie? I've got no investment. I don't give anything remotely resembling a fuck. I have *heard the reports*.

Those girls are lying, I said, because he's so handsome. They want it to be true. But he doesn't like vaginas.

I think he's quite fond of them, actually. She rammed another cake slice into her mouth and mumbled, The red flags are flying from the battlements.

After dinner he stood on the badly lit smoking porch with a paperback spread open in his long fingers. The book looked serious: there was no picture on the front. So diligent, my Julian, trying to keep his brain alive in this illiterate circus tent. A herd of girls kept interrupting him with their snorts and whinnies. Whatcha reading? Check out Mr. Intellectualist, he reads standing up, Jesus.

It's called *Diss-see-muh-nation*.

Ooh, is it about semen?

Julian smiled. In a way. In a remote way.

I like books about semen.

Me too. Who wrote it?

A French philosopher, he said darkly.

The admiring gaggle flocked closer, smothering him, until he shut the book. I listened sadly from the other end of the porch. He should not allow himself to be distracted. He should steel himself against those vaginas. If I were his boyfriend I'd let him read in peace. If I were his boyfriend I would admit that I had finished only two semesters at Eau Claire Community College, and ask him to tutor me in the life of the mind, stretch out beside him while he read the semen book aloud.

Just after curfew there was a knock on our door. Chuckie, swathed in sweatshirt, scarf, and jeans despite the overheating radiators—he made sure to keep his body covered at all times—went to open it. What's up, Little Professor?

Where's Timothy?

I was under the covers, reading a book my counselor had given me about people who love too much. I shoved the book down toward my feet and affected a sleepy grin.

Chuckie looked suspiciously from me to Julian, then sidled out of the room. Julian sat boldly at the end of my bed. The fact of his body on the blanket, alone with mine, made my teeth start to chatter.

I have a naughty plan, he said.

What's that?

Mexico, he said.

Mexico?

As in, let's go.

Oh!

I'm sure we can find a cheap flight, he went on. I'm sick of these Midwestern skies. I want sun, I want decadence.

It would be hard to stay sober in Mexico, I said.

He just kept smiling.

Oh, I said.

You down?

I guess. I mean, yes!

All right then, he said. Tell no one. Especially not your fat little friend. We'll make the arrangements tomorrow.

But what will. . . .

Sleep tight, sweet thing! He tapped his finger on the tip of my nose and departed.

When Chuckie came back in he made a glancing search of the room for evidence of hasty grappling.

It was awful not telling Ginna. I wanted to flaunt the proof of Julian's devotion. The secret was too delicious to keep, but I kept it. I floated through the day under a Mexican sun—I could feel its heat, even as the snow began dropping after lunch and fell until dinnertime, when the people with jobs came trudging back to the house. Julian was one of the last to arrive. I was waiting discreetly by the fish tank. He unwrapped his red scarf, shook melting flakes from his hair, and gave me a tantalizing purse of the lips.

We're set, he whispered. I made some calls. There's just one minor hitch.

Hitch?

Cash for the tickets. I'm totally dry at the moment. If you could front my half, I'd pay you back as soon as my parents stop detaching with love. I think they're coming around. Shouldn't be long now.

I asked how much. He said two grand. That seemed like a lot for plane tickets to a country that was right next to our country.

Sounds cool, I said, except for I don't have a job and—

But your father's an attorney, is he not?

How did you know that?

You told me. Didn't you tell me?

The bell rang shrilly from the cafeteria, launching a wave of bodies out of the lounge. See what you can do, murmured Julian, brushing a wayward clump of hair off my forehead. Because Mexico is a great deal more romantic than this here little panopticon.

Our cul-de-sac lay just off West Seventh, the artery between downtown and the airport. It was a long, grubby street of package stores and Super Americas. Air was foulest near the river, by the breweries, where yeast settled in the clouds. Smokestacks rose wisping behind the rooftops of sad houses that clustered on the side streets. On the corner of West Seventh and Juno was a dealership called Timberwolf New & Used. My father was going to kill me, but he wouldn't actually kill me. He'd be angry for a while, and bring up the name of my mother, who would be turning in her box. Hadn't I done enough to disgrace her. Wasn't it bad enough to get arrested on the sidewalk in front of that goddamn sodomy farm. (It's a dance club, Dad.) What were you doing with all those goddamn pills, are you some kind of idiot? (They weren't even mine. Another guy's I was holding them for.)

By the time he learned of my departure I would be in

Mexico, maybe never to return. You could live in Mexico very cheaply, I'd been told. Julian would read philosophy in Spanish and I would cook feasts of spiced cornmeal and guava leaves. It would never be cold. Julian could teach me the proper positions. My inexperience would delight him, thrust him into the starring role. Our skins would turn brown and gorgeous. We'd drink tequila if we felt like it, but never to excess.

The Timberwolf man did a fast appraisal and returned to the office looking wary. This vehicle is in pretty good condition, he said. Why you getting rid of it?

My mother's sick. Her coverage won't pay for the extra medication.

Show me them papers again? He scanned the title and insurance and my driver's license a few more times. Twenty-one's the best I can do, he said eventually.

That will be fine, sir, I said, as my stomach fizzed and crinkled.

I offered to accompany Julian to the travel agent's, but he would not hear of it. Honey, you've done enough! he purred, tucking the cashier's check into his chain wallet. Your footwork is over. Time to relax. Take a nap—snuggle under. By the time you wake up I'll have the tickets.

It was Saturday, the longest and bleakest day at the house. There was nothing scheduled. Nothing to do except watch sports in the lounge or go sit in a coffee shop. I usually slept for most of Saturday, but now I couldn't. In the waiting my eyes wouldn't close; once he had set off, in his red scarf and adorable boots, I started pacing around the house. There was a rough game of spades in progress near the fish tank. A girl was weeping on the phone by the laundry room. In the stairwell off the dining room, Vincent and Anne Sarah were locked in embrace.

73

I found Ginna at her usual post, sampling a special weekend item—sticky buns—and reading a pamphlet entitled *Get Busy Living: How to Thrive, Not Just Survive, Without Chemicals*.

Are you learning great things? I asked.

Many great things. Such pleasures await me as, page three, *taking long walks in the sunshine with a friend*. Want one? She nodded back at the tray of gleaming buns.

I have no appetite.

Still lovesick?

I smiled and nudged the secret back into my mouth.

You'll be on your own with that fruitless project as of Monday.

Monday?

My out date, she said. I am gone, released. Weren't you aware of this?

This Monday? Where will you go?

Ginna narrowed her eyes, then rolled them. I *told* you, that studio above the video store. The month-to-month. You're going to help me decorate. *Remember?*

Oh right! (But I would be in Mexico.) I'll miss you, I said. I really will.

It's practically down the street. All you'll have to miss is how pretty I look first thing in the morning, before I put my contacts in.

By dinnertime I was worried. It was snowing again, which had maybe made the streets impassable, stranding Julian at the travel agent's. Are we having a blizzard? I asked the night tech. That snow looks fierce.

A few inches tops, he said witheringly.

Our ranks were small in the cafeteria. Attendance at weekend meals wasn't mandatory, and the only people who ate at the house on Saturdays were the people who couldn't think of any-place better to go, or who were too depressed to drag themselves to a place even if they could think of one. I stuffed myself with rolls. The pork loin didn't look bad, or the mashed potatoes either, but I stuck exclusively to bread, slathered it with butter, hoped the spongy flour would soak up some of the acid in my stomach. Ginna, who couldn't see the acid or the worry press-ing against the backs of my eyes, struggled to get her mouth around a towering sandwich of pork, potatoes, mustard greens, and mayonnaise. Drips of potato flecked her chin.

On a break between bites she asked could I drive her things over to the new apartment on Monday. A formality, this asking, since she knew I would—or would have, if I still owned a car. Sure, I said, seeing no reason to notify her of the car's disappearance. By Monday she'd have read my farewell letter, with its heartfelt wishes of luck, its promise to send postcards from sun-drenched villages. She would understand, if not at first, then over time. She was my friend and wanted me to be happy. Take it wherever you can get it, she liked to say of happiness, because it's not hanging from a whole lot of trees. I'd told her she ought to publish these wise sayings and live off the royalties.

At midnight the tech locked the front doors and read the sign-out sheet to see who had broken curfew. Where have all the flowers gone? he asked the air. *Graciela B.: movie. Liam O.: shopping. Julian Q.: search for meaning.*

Liam pounded on the thick glass doors a few minutes after twelve. The tech let him in and said he was grounded for one week.

But, like, no way, protested Liam. My watch says five of.

Of no consequence, said the tech. Mine says four past.

But it's so not my fault. I *thought* I was on time. How can I

75

get grounded for having a cheap watch? What is this, the Fourth Reich?

Welcome to Bergen-Belsen, said the tech.

I find that incredibly offensive, called Ginna from the couch, where we were cuddled under blankets watching a murder mystery set in an elf-ridden Welsh village.

The tech ignored her.

Anne Frank *died* at Bergen-Belsen, she insisted. You don't just go bandying that word about.

Who's Anne Frank? asked Jerome.

It had stopped snowing. Our lawn lay glittering, a pale sea spreading from the rails of the smoking porch, where I went to stand vigil. I waited until one. Until two. Until I couldn't feel my feet. I saw police cars surrounding him—a bus hitting him—the snow swamping him under a great white weight. These scenarios played in vibrant colors on the ice-screen of the lawn. Julian's body getting crunched by a taxi meant I was not a total fool. Julian's limbs ripped from his torso by vultures meant my expectations had been reasonable. Julian rushing to make curfew, sprinting across the train tracks near our cul-de-sac, deaf to the locomotive's horn, the tickets burning in his pocket—bam!—tickets now shredded, like his flesh, by the shrieking wheels, meant I hadn't been suckered.

Oh, but I had.

At three A.M. I climbed back down to my room. Chuckie was snoring in the light of both lamps. I went to sleep in my clothes.

Tonight, said the head counselor, we say good-bye to a resident who has successfully completed our program—let's hear it for Ginna W.!

We clapped, and some nice things were said by the other

counselors. A shiny medallion was pressed into Ginna's palm with cheerful instructions to *stay the course*. She blushed and muttered.

When the happy moment was over, and Ginna had thudded back down next to me by the bubbler, the head counselor stopped smiling. We are also bidding adieu, he said, to some people who have *not* been successful at obeying the rules of this community. I am sorry to announce that Arnold P. and Timothy T. are being discharged for noncompliance with employment expectations.

A hum of interest rippled the crowd. Those who had been sleeping during Ginna's ceremony lifted their heads. Bad news was the most reliable source of entertainment at the house. I searched for Arnold's face, found it, saw no change upon it. His mouth sat in its usual sneer. He had pride; I would have some too. Tears were pinching my eyeballs but I didn't need to let them fall.

The head counselor was not finished. As many of you already know, Julian and Graciela did not come home last night and have, of course, been discharged in absentia. Not a stellar weekend for our community. I hope the rest of you will take some time to reflect on the consequences your peers are facing, so that such consequences need not be visited on your heads in the future.

Our community dispersed to smoke and play cards. Arnold and I were taken into the office to sign papers. This is bullshit, remarked Arnold calmly.

I said nothing, because the tears were too close.

Julian laughing as he cashed the check.

Graciela neighing at his side.

The hatchback being steered across dried cow pies by a farmer's hammy knuckles. My mother rotating in her box. My father—

Has been notified, the tech told me. Mentioned something about the last straw. Said you could damn well sleep in your car for the time being.

Least you *have* one, spat Arnold. It's back to the streets for me, motherfuck.

Spare us, said the tech.

The next morning Ginna's suitcases were waiting by the fish tank. I put my duffel bag next to them and sat down on the carpet. Arnold and his luggage had already been whisked away by a woman in a pink truck.

Johnnycake, returning from breakfast, told me to get up off the floor. Muster some dignity, he said. You got a lotta more years to live, boy. Start making use.

I will, I said from the floor.

Then stand *up*. Greet the day. Where you headed from here?

I don't know.

Shut up with the forlorn, he said. You be fine. Get a job while you still have your health.

I'm ready! yelled Ginna from down the hall. Start the engines! She came up smoothing an enormous plaid shirt down over her thighs. Good-bye, Johnnycake. They hugged. He looked at me, debating, then chose an enthusiastic handshake.

Ginna, I said as we dragged our bags toward the parking lot, there is no more engine.

What?

Let's take the bus.

The bus stop is *seven blocks away*. Where the fuck's your car?

Got towed, I said. (Guilt.) Stolen, actually. (More guilt.) No, I sold it.

She just looked at me for a little while, then put her suit-cases down, went back into the house, and came out again two minutes later. I called a cab, which you can pay for with some of your cash bounty.

The cash is not exactly bountiful, I said.

Oh, God—what'd you do—offer to subsidize Julian and Graciela's honeymoon at Ye Olde Shooting Gallerie Bed & Breakfast?

Possibly so, I admitted.

Ginna's new home was on the second floor above Fantasy Video. It was clean, except for the bathtub, and her morning commute was now five seconds long. Month to month, she reminded herself out loud to stave off the sadness of living in a tiny wood-paneled room overlooking an alley above the adult video store where you work. Totally temporary.

Temporary, I echoed, armed with bleach and paper towels. I had offered to deal with the bathtub, which was encrusted with unidentified brown-red matter. While I scrubbed she sat on the toilet, smoking, and lectured me about my stupidity. You're a nice person, she said, and thus you assume other people are nice too. They are not. Most people are not nice at all. You have to act accordingly.

Isn't that kind of depressing?

Not as depressing as being robbed blind by a trifling poseur.

God bless him, I said feebly.

Moving along. New subject. Let's think of where to have dinner tonight. To celebrate. Toast our new freedom. Free of the house, free of trifling poseurs. . . .

Free of car, I added.

After the sun went down, we woke up hungry from our naps on a sleeping bag and a folded blanket. The Copper Dome

Restaurant was two blocks away, an acceptable walking distance for Ginna, and specialized in thirteen varieties of pancake. I had original buckwheat, she had banana chocolate chunk. We did not talk about the future. Did not discuss my staying or going. My father was not mentioned, nor Ginna's mother, who often asked Ginna wasn't it enough to have been plunged into these reduced circumstances—did she have to be getting fat in the bargain?

On the walk back, flakes caught on our lashes. The floor of the city sparkled quietly. The snow would stop, and morning would come. Ginna would go downstairs to stand behind the smut counter while I drank the coffee she had cooked on the two-ringed stove. The air would be cold against the blurry panes. And I would make the call to my father, who sat worrying in Wisconsin, and give him more reasons to be disappointed.

But the sacrificed car and my hasty departure were better things to tell him than nothing at all, than a frightening silence, than long days of wondering where I slept at night. *I have a roof,* I planned to say, *for now. I have a friend. For now it's all right. I will let you know what happens.*

THIEVES AND MAPMAKERS

On the last day I saw my mother, we ate dinner on the back porch. Veal chops and butter beans and apricots in syrup. Flies swarmed around the fruit but my mother said to ignore them, so we chewed and chewed and she asked about work. My job was at the fairgrounds, running the Demon Cups. I would listen to the kids scream for three minutes then pull the lever back. I watched for accidents.

I don't like it, I told her.

Oh, well, you do! she said, popping a fly-pocked apricot into her mouth.

I don't like the job.

But you do like the job.

The calm in her voice made me tired. That summer I was tired all the time. My spine had twisted into knots from the tedium of running up my body. My eyes ached from looking at things I had already seen. I had an unnamed sickness that scaled my skin and brittled my eyeballs, but being sick was more pleasurable than being bored and I felt more interesting, in my affliction, than my mother and the neighbors content with their strong lungs and straight spines and useless health.

I believed the Town itself had infected me. Although it looked clean on the surface, it was like a river that's quit running, whose water languishes on the rocks, collecting germs. Because nothing in the Town ever changed shape, hidden viruses were allowed to grow. The rooms of my house stank of sameness; the familiar pall of the slipcovers had become a daily torment. It wasn't city, it wasn't country, it was a way station of gray streets and brown storefronts and paralyzed faces.

In those hot guts of August I would wake up drenched with fears of waking in the Town until I died. My sweat smelled like rust.

On the day I turned eleven, I had asked why my father was missing from yet another of my birthday parties. My mother explained that when he left, four winters before, *he never did find his way back to us.* I imagined my father coughing up knobs of phlegm, hobbled by gangrene, heels printing blood in the snow, unable to find the right road. Like my father, most Town natives got swallowed up by the outside world if they agreed to step into it. Kids off to college stayed away for good; two-week vacations turned into permanent leaves; fortune-seekers, once departed, were rarely seen again. As a result, the Town's population was dwindling steadily. One of the high schools had already been shut down. The dentists had moved away for lack of patients and we walked around with bad teeth.

After the birthday cake was gone I found a state map and stared at the little square south of Springfield that the Town was supposed to occupy. The space lay empty. The Town was not listed in the index. I was shocked to learn, at eleven years of age, that I did not live anywhere. I told myself there had been an error at the map factory and from that point on scrutinized every map I could get ahold of, assuming there must be some record of our existence. I worked diligently to collect them— stained scrolls from antique stores, cheap laminates from gas stations—and pasted them into notebooks. I had maps from every continent, world atlases and national cartographs I'd sent away for. If I had to live in an invisible city I wanted at least to own charted proof of places that did exist.

At the Laundromat I found Lily. We had been meeting there almost every night of the summer to buy coffees and spend quarters on pinball. Our patterns of migration were reliable.

I heard a kid say there's something happening at the Y.

Like what, I said.

Something, I don't know, who cares? Finish this. Lily handed me the coffee cup and snapped open her compact and we drove lipstick on. We look fucking smashing! she declared and we ran down the slope behind the Laundromat to cut across the park, the wind lifting our dresses.

The YMCA gym usually stayed empty, but that night its windows were blazing when we walked up. A handful of kids had collected at the door's mouth. Lily and I took our place among them, those kids in brown lace-up shoes and denim jackets who shared with us the same bad luck of getting born nowhere.

It's a concert, one of them said.

There had never been a concert in the Town. Live music only happened if there was a wedding.

A charcoal van plowed up the drive and four boys stepped out. They might have been angels, weird as they looked to us. We stared at their two-colored hair, stiff with pomade, and at the four matching black bullrings in their sunburnt noses. (No one had seen a bullring except in magazines; none among us had ever attempted one, not even the kids who tattooed calligraphy on their knuckles or carved symbols into their forearms with heated-up knives.) These boys wore long velvet coats, studded belts, striped trousers with buttons at the calf, and box-heeled boots you couldn't have purchased within a three-hundred mile radius of where they now stood.

Like pirates, breathed Lily.

Inside the gym, a red glow from the exit signs turned their bodies into black paper cutouts. While they fussed with the amplifiers we waited dutifully, grateful for this unexplained gift of disruption.

Their music was tuneless and played at volumes so high the notes could not separate themselves and were left for dead under the static. I could not pretend to like it, but I was enthralled. The gunfire decibels, the stuttering howls, their dripping mouths, the grisly discomfort of the chords: together it announced, in no uncertain terms, *Your life is not happy and neither is mine.* Inside the frantic noise the singer hovered and slouched, spitting out wails at random and only opening his eyes between songs, to scan the meager audience, to lift his chin at us. He was the only one I watched. He was not good-looking in the way singers are supposed to be. As a little boy he had probably been winsome and soft-eyed—poised to grow into a handsome man—but now his face was bruisey, gutted. I imagined his parents' dismay as they watched his skin go bad, his eyes shrink to slits. There were traces of boyish beauty underneath the wreckage, so faint they served only to magnify the beauty's vanishing. Yet he possessed a quality more attractive—to me—than handsomeness: it was his sheer haggardness, the battered-ship's-hull look he wore, as if a lifetime of senseless routines had etched gulleys in his cheeks.

He looked sicker than I felt.

After the applause, everyone shifted weight in embarrassment, still dumbfounded as to why these creatures had come into our midst. The singer barked into the microphone: We are collecting donations, as much as you can give, please dig deep because we are far from home and need gas money. Thank you!

He picked up a coffee can and began making the rounds. Lily rifled through her plastic purse for quarters. God, I wish I had more. Only got two-seventy-five here. . . .

I'm not giving them anything, I said.

But you have to! she hissed. They came all this way.

Well, they're making a mint off everyone else.

I had been watching my schoolmates hand them dollar bills, even fives—for a few minutes of bad music—and sensed keenly the not-so-veiled insult in it, the pirates' assumption that we, a group of shambling hicks, would happily fork over our last coins for the pleasure of their company.

When the singer got to us, Lily cast her eyes down and whimpered, Y'all played really badass.

Thank you, madam, he said briskly, holding out the can to me.

Come on, said Lily. Give him something.

I'm broke, I said.

Oh really, said the singer. Or is it just you didn't like us? Got more of a taste for country music?

No, I don't like country.

He smiled, took a flask from his jacket, and unscrewed it. You know what, neither do I.

I smiled back, sipping from the proffered flask. It hurt my throat. Somebody turned on the gym lights and we all looked around anxiously.

Guess it's time, the singer said, to take our leave.

In their van, my ears rang from the music and the large amounts of whiskey made available to me by Squinch. (I wondered what kind of regular name his mother had given him.) I looked around for Lily, convinced she had been with me the whole time, but through the smeared glass I saw the lawn abandoned, the parking lot empty. Squinch was slumped against the door with a dyed-blue forelock hanging across his cheek. Beside him squatted the drummer, scowling as he counted money from the can. Not the most lucrative shit hole, he muttered. Remind me never to book a show in Springfield again.

This is not Springfield, I said.

Where the hell is it, then?

Springfield's forty miles—

You're lying.

No.

The drummer hollered, Which one of you fuckwits booked this show?

They bickered for a few minutes before losing interest in the fact that they had come here to take our money entirely by accident. I wanted to tell them to get a good look around since they'd never be able to find this place again.

The other boys clambered up into the seats to prepare for departure and I was light-headed with envy at what they had in store: new roads, strange cities, a different sun rising each morning. They were going, they said, to New Orleans. A big show awaited them there.

Squinch slid his fingers through a rip in my stocking, rested a nail briefly against my thigh, then ventured his whole hand through and promised to buy me new stockings any color I wanted. He began whispering things. The drummer had started the engine, which sputtered so grievously I couldn't hear a word.

My mother abandoned us, he shrieked. Me and my sisters all under the age of six, she just took off. I think she lives in California now.

Water stood in his eyes, but it wasn't tears.

I shouted that I was sorry.

He grinned and asked if I had any room in my heart for a motherless boy. I shrugged, drunk. Hey fellows, Squinch yelled up to them, I like this little one. I think we might take her. You'd like to get stolen, wouldn't you?

We drove. It was black and starless. Even in my stupor I was careful to memorize the route, the exact roads taken, the billboards and landmarks passed, because I needed to chart with precision any venture that took me away from the Town. It was bolstering to know the details of my whereabouts outside a place that was not anywhere. I had my backpack which held the drugstore notebook sticky with glue and shreds of maps; as soon as there was light to see by I would sketch in a new one, the one I was drawing in my head, fat black lines between stars-for-towns dipping across blue lines for rivers and the van itself a bright red circle flying down the page, destined for locations I had only seen on other maps.

I must have slept. The van still throttled along but now everything was steeped in glare and the waxing heat of midmorning. There were mountains on our right and the road reached ahead into a little valley with colors more vivid than any I had witnessed at home: dazzling aquas and limes, rich muddy reds, the gleamy transparent silver of the air itself. It was like watching a movie. The gray-scale filter I was used to had been lifted clean.

Where are we? I asked Squinch. He had his head on my thigh and was smoking with his eyes closed.

I don't know. Every highway on earth looks the same, he added mournfully, as you will soon discover.

•

I learned that these pirates were plagued by their own special sort of illness. The only foods they could stand to eat were potatoes and toasted bread products. They got nauseous at the mention of vegetables or anything that came from an animal. Instead of eating they plied their stomachs with stay-awake medicine. On the floor of the van, spilled coffee had soaked into little wax packets and powder-flecked ziplocks. All four boys, I noticed, were twitching constantly, glancing around with fretful eyes. This agitation made me feel closer to them. Their translucent skin, the dried sputum at the corners of their mouths, and the way their shrunken muscles hung as if ready to come off the bone meant they were nothing like the normal people I'd grown up with. I started laughing from the pleasure of being among people who had something wrong with them. Squinch looked at me suspiciously, maybe thinking I was crazy because I laughed at nothing but was so quiet the rest of the time. I assumed he had seen plenty of lunatics in his travels and would prefer them, in their illness, to the lackluster of the healthy sane.

The night sky was lanced by lightning, shards of wind. We waited on the thunder in the asphalt lot behind a truckstop cafeteria and the boys placed wagers (size of storm, duration of storm, what particular shit might get fucked up by storm). Innocent rapture crinkled their snouts. The water hammered dents in the roof of the van. Squinch jumped out and dragged me with him into the soak, dancing off-balance, threatening to relieve my arm of its socket.

In the men's room we dripped and shivered. He lifted me onto the sink—the gun-mouth faucet at the small of my back— and hoisted my legs around him, gnawing my collarbone, snorting and giggling. He pinched my breasts between his fingers and said, Love of Christ they're so little!

Cold beads of humiliation sprang up on my cheeks; I kept my eyes on the ceiling.

But then your nipples, he went on in a surgeon's voice, are the longest I ever saw.

Holding him there, bracing my leg muscles so he wouldn't fall, I calculated the distance I had traveled from home.

He clawed at the buttons of his shirt. This is my heart, he instructed, pressing me to listen against his damp chest. I felt the ridges meet my cheek: knobby, corrugated flesh.

I drew back, forgetting not to breathe, and gagged at the urine waft. What's that?

Well, love, it's a little scar, you see. Thick and bruise-colored, a crosshatch of notched lumps, it stretched from sternum to armpit. A frayed black thread poked out from one end (the stitches, still intact), and looking closer I noticed that the hewn sheaths of skin on either side had not grown together, instead relying wholly on the black thread to secure them.

Don't be scared, Squinch said.

But.

It doesn't hurt me.

But.

It's cool if you touch it. I'd *like* you to touch it. He held my fingertip and moved it lightly over the fibrous bumps. Just whatever you do, love. . . . I sat unbreathing. Never, *ever* pull the thread. Promise not to?

Yes.

Say it.

I promise.

Good girl.

Then he found his way into me and stayed there for a

minute or two. I stared at the sooty green tiles on the opposite wall, waiting for what would happen, not feeling anything beyond a cautious pressure. He withdrew and whispered, Good girl and buttoned his shirt.

I kept track of our coordinates in the notebook. The name of each town we passed through was entered into my ledger, the villages of Missouri and Arkansas and Tennessee and Mississippi inscribed in back-slanted lettering. I would wake up before the others and make a map of the day before. We would be bunched up in the van or splayed across couches in a fourteen-year-old's parents' basement, and it would be late in the morning when regular people have already arrived at their regular jobs and are following the dreary mandate of proper living. The boys, like good invalids, slept their choked sleeps well into the afternoon and allowed me time to commit our journey to paper. With colored pencils I sketched the scenery. Drought-cooked riverbeds littered with birds' skeletons; three tiny sisters on a Memphis sidewalk rigged up in Elvis costumes lip-synching to a tape of "Blue Suede Shoes"; a road of roofless houses, acting as if nothing had happened to them, their backyards fluttering with clean laundry.

During the final stretch through Louisiana, a warm rain fell. We drove along in it, all of us twisted up in unnatural positions to prevent our moist calves from touching one another, until without warning Squinch pulled over into the mud, flung the door open, and bowed his blue head. Raindrops sprayed against his thighs. He drew ragged breaths, mimicking the death-rattle, held his hands to his ears and rocked back and forth.

These theatrics persisted until Rabb nudged me, hissing, Somebody else's got to drive.

Crawling out from the piles of backpacks and drum shells I caught my dress on the door ashtray; at the sound of its ripping they all laughed gleefully. Squinch stretched out in the passenger seat, his fit subsiding as suddenly as it had begun.

The rain had cleared by the time we crossed the swamps into New Orleans. Through the gloom I steered, teeth chattering with fatigue, past crumbling balustrades, sunken lawns, glittering vines that crawled up the walls of ornate and dismal houses lying still under the heat. The boys, accustomed to milder mid-Atlantic summers, sweated madly in their vintage jackets but were too vain to remove them. I had come to fear their vanity, the relish with which these pirates fondled their silken trousers as they slid them on and the hours spent oiling the thorns of their hair and examining themselves in the rearview mirror, cigarettes dangling from their mouths. I knew that when Squinch gave me his sunglasses to wear, it was in order to see his reflection in them when he bent to kiss me.

On a street that frothed with palm trees and pink flowers, we pulled up to the Mausoleum, home of Bill Bones— renowned on tour circuits, said the boys, for his excellent parties and encyclopedic knowledge of musical history. Opening the door was a pale, red-eyed stick in sweatpants who trembled as he whispered, What time is it?

Uh. . . .

Don't receive callers before three. Come back later.

But we're the band.

Did you nawt hear me? Back at three! And the door closed resolutely, shuddering on its hinges.

We found a café on a street of gas stations. The waiter stood in martyrdom while the boys complained there was nothing but eggs on the menu. Squinch snapped, Just bring us some fucking coffee please because we can't eat any of this chickenshit! and five minutes later, fueled, they fled the café in a blur of black legs and white arms whirled with skulls and ships and fire. I paid the bill and was ridiculed for it afterward in the dim bar where the boys drank Hurricanes steadily for the next several hours.

We got back to the Mausoleum just as cocktail hour was beginning. There was an array of guests from the city's gutter-boudoirs: Mrs. Julius, the thirteen-year-old palm reader; a few strippers whose specialty was the Lapped Catholic Schoolgirls ensemble piece; a dance-hall drag queen with delicate green veins crisscrossing her cheeks; several Mohicaned squatters; a certified public accountant; a runaway from Jackson, Mississippi who had been wearing the same T-shirt for nineteen days; and a brooding man in sharkskin who claimed to have taught a famous singer everything he knew about pain during the singer's salad days in New Orleans.

For strange people, they were strangely calm. To my eyes, used to the colorless faces and slate-lit backdrop of the Town, these guests were exotic, yet they sat with their legs crossed and were careful to ash in the ashtrays and didn't scream or shout. I waited to be spoken to. Bill Bones stood at a marble sideboard in the mildew-stained dining room pouring blue and purple cordials into stemmed plastics. The drinks were so pretty that nobody mentioned how bad they tasted.

Shading her eyes against the glint from the cups, Mrs. Julius asked politely, What do you do?—her eyes fixed on my earlobes instead of my face.

I'm a traveler, I answered.

Oh, I see.

Among the late arrivals to cocktail hour was a girl with hair of pinkish chrome who laughed a lot and kept fiddling with the bead purse on her lap. When Squinch was introduced to her he couldn't mask his interest. Drool glistered on his cuspids.

Pleased to, you know, meet you, he said.

You're the rock star?

Some people think so. You coming to the show this evening?

Maybe. If there's time. The girl, who was called Astrid, yawned. Where are you from?

New York City, ma'am! Squinch paused to allow time for this falsehood to sink in. It's the only place big enough, really, if you know—

You're from the city? That's strange, I used to live there but I never heard of—

Well it's not strange if you think about how many bands are—

It doesn't matter. She took a cigarette from her purse, which prompted Squinch to strike a a match for her. The flame died before she could get a light from it.

Sorry, he mumbled, wiping back his forelock.

In the vacant hour before it was time to head for the club, Squinch cornered Astrid in an upstairs room. I watched by the door. I looked to see where she put her hands. They kissed standing up for a few minutes, thrashing mechanically against each other. When he hitched up her lace dress she batted him away and coughed.

I love this dress, he blithered, undeterred. It's like, you know, like gossamer. . . . And your hair is. . . . Your hair, baby, is the coolest.

This thing? Astrid seized a hank of it and slid it off her head. Her skull, a dimpled egg, was studded with tiny black bristles.

Squinch gaped. A lady of surprises! He kissed her again and said, And are you really a boy underneath all that?

She spat out his saliva. Oh, come on.

Because you can show me, sweetie. And if you show me, I'll show you—

I'm bored, she announced. 'M going down to get another drink.

I retreated into shadow to let her pass and saw, without having to look, Squinch standing bewildered on the broken floorboards.

The club was gouged out beneath a Chinese restaurant, with black walls and barbed wire around the stage and a huge, unnecessary fire crackling in a brick fireplace. Fifty people in mesh and leatherette were knocking back drinks. And so the boys played, I'm guessing, though I don't remember the music; I couldn't notice much beyond the incredible discomfort of standing in that boiling room. Everyone's makeup was running hard and it was too hot to form a thought. The whole thing seemed depressing, the darkness and the drone and the people getting wasted exactly as they would the next night and for years of nights to come. I wanted—though the wanting concerned me, it meant I wasn't as sick as I had presumed—to be someplace clean. I had been dizzy for three days straight and I did not want to be dizzy, nor did I particularly want to feel my stomach shriveling and throbbing from a diet of black coffee and potato chips and powdered medicines.

When I searched out the bathroom for a splash of water, hoping it might bring back some of the blood to my face, somebody was throwing up in the stall. I leaned against the door listening to the heaves. Astrid emerged, wiping her mouth and eyes. She was wearing a different wig—red, shimmery, straight to her chin.

Hi kid, she rasped. What's new.

It made sense for Squinch to prefer such a girl, such an obviously tougher and sicker girl than I.

I pushed my way through the mirthless oven back up to the surface, where I waited on the curb until the show ended. Afterward I crouched behind a dumpster to watch Squinch while the boys loaded out the equipment. He was scratching inside his trousers, his hair had collapsed under the weight of sweat, and, unaware he was being observed, he had allowed his face to fall back into its natural lines: not sad or sick, not death's-door theatrical, not anything but tired.

All the cabinets are in, Rabb called to him. And Teddy's getting the money.

I need to take a dump before we leave, all right? He sloped off and Rabb just stood there, yawning, with his hands in his pockets.

We returned to the Mausoleum. Until six or seven in the morning the house was full of people who looked exactly like the people in the club but might have been different people. Mrs. Julius was there, asking again what did I do. Squinch told her I was on summer vacation and Mrs. Julius said, Oh, I see and Squinch added that it was past both our bedtimes.

When the sun was up and burning and the guests had cleared away, we settled down on the carpets of the parlor. I dreamed of the Town, of its odors: the first cold day in fall, when all lingering frowses of heat have left the air and the newly emptied chill is flecked with wood smoke, soft and bitter, the smell of anticipation; and springtime—bright, forgiving air with the hint of unannounced visitors, impending journeys. Of course no visitors ever showed and no journeys were ever taken and the smell would soon retreat, replaced by a dingy warmth. This was why the Town disappointed me so badly: it could never deliver on the promise of its scents.

Squinch was gnashing his teeth in his sleep and it interrupted my dream. The others slept on, open-mouthed. I went to squat beside him and peeled up his grimy shirt. For almost an hour I sat in wait, staring at the swollen scar.

When I pulled the stitching free, the mottled skin parted willingly. Squinch did not even flinch. There was a faint hissing—the release of air and gas from their confines, a waft of blood smell that stung my eyes—and I peered in to see the muscle itself, its chambers and arteries athrob: but there was no heart nestled there. It was only a pocket of dried flesh clinging to the ribs, sprinkled with black, spent veins. I put a finger to the wall of flesh and it was stiff.

I felt the rush of terror he had intended for me and for anyone else who saw it. I doubted I was the first girl to taste the acid on her tongue, the dread and panic and mistrust of her own eyes. I would have screamed but was afraid of his reddish lids opening. After the shock faded, I noticed that something did not look right. Something about this fantastic mess was not fantastic enough. Swallowing hard, I pressed my knuckles into the wound. The gouge was shallower than it looked. And there was a pulse underneath.

Motherless he might be; heartless he wasn't. I wondered what sort of instruments had been used, and how much medicine Squinch had had to eat beforehand, and if he'd even dared to execute the procedure himself. I expected he hadn't; he was not so brave. Somebody else had been called upon to make him appear gruesome.

I fumbled with the thread. All I had was the bobby pin holding back my hair, so I tied the end of it to the damp yarn, sent up a prayer, and shoved the pin into one of the crusted holes. Squinch's shoulders jerked but he went on sleeping. I sewed and sewed, fetching sparks of blood, but there was not really so much blood, after all, and I was pleased with my handiwork. I licked the scar clean and pulled his shirt back down.

By the time Bill Bones woke the boys, I had convinced myself Squinch wouldn't notice. I was proud to have covered up my disobedience so tidily.

Astrid came downstairs brushing long yellow curls and wiping her mouth and eyes.

Will you breakfast with us, my lady? Squinch asked her. Standing there in a T-shirt, rubbing the pimples on his withered arms, he did not look dashing: there was too much sunlight in the room.

Astrid directed us to a pancake house. Though I'd barely slept and was dizzier than ever, I ate with relish and ordered a second helping of silver dollars, turning over the secret in my mind.

Strumpet's got syrup all over her mitts, remarked Squinch indulgently. He took a napkin and began wiping my hands.

Rabb asked, How many hours to Mobile?

Between two and twenty. And your turn to drive. Squinch stopped wiping, squinted down. What have we got here?

I folded my hands in my lap and said, I'm full now.

Give those back to me. He frowned. I wonder where you've been poking these. . . .

I saw the tiny caked smear on the pad of my index finger. He dipped the napkin in a water glass and rubbed at the spot. It wouldn't come off.

Hey Squinchs, can I finish your home fries?

Squinch raised his head and told Teddy coldly, No, you can't. We are leaving.

Still gripping my hand, he led us out with the practiced casualness of nonpaying customers who wish to exit restaurants unnoticed.

I have to go to the bathroom, I whispered in the parking lot. Go on, then.

But if she goes back in, they're going to—

Shut up. Go ahead, sweetheart! and Squinch smiled into the pools of his sunglasses.

In the ladies' room I scraped at the finger, but the red refused to come off. The skin began to ache. Astrid sidled in. She took my cheeks in her hands and asked, What are you doing?

I backed away. Nothing. I just—

I mean, what are you doing following these jackasses around? Please explain it to me.

I'm not following.

Then what, precisely, are you up to?

Traveling.

Not so much anymore.

What do—

They're leaving without you. In fact, they *left*.

I thought: He's carried me this far.

Astrid continued, And he said, I quote: *Bride deserves her punishment.*

Why didn't he ask *you* to go?

He did, last night, at the fireplace place.

They're going to Alabama next.

I've been to Alabama before, she shrugged. Don't plan to go again.

Why not?

Astrid looked at me like she was seeing me for the first time. She lit two cigarettes and handed one over; it smelled like burnt sugar. Are you going to go home?

I can't, I said.

Is that so.

Yeah.

Why don't you go to California?

Is it nice there?

Not necessarily, she said, but people go.

I had maps of California. I knew the mileage from Los Angeles to Mexico. I'd read books about people hopping trains to get to the coast. I don't think I want to go to California, I admitted.

Astrid paid for a cab that dropped us in front of a café where, she explained, you could sit for as long as you liked without buying anything. Then she said good-bye and went off with her blonde curls swinging.

I sat without buying anything and leafed through my notebook and inspected my finger, which was as clean as the day I was born. The blood had sweated off, the indelible stain erased. We were not like the fairy tale, as hard as he'd tried to make it so.

WASTE N? TIME
IF THIS METH?D FAILS

He is the cutest at the franzy house.

He can hold his breath for three minutes.

He lies on his stomach when he pictures the fish-stick girl, so his roommate can't hear.

He likes to watch salt dry in bronchial patterns.

He dislikes improv comedy.

He laughs when the mailman falls on the ice.

He cries when a penny is removed from his nose.

He is thirty-one years old.

He knows who the president is, but not why.

He wrapped his arms around the choking man like he loved him.

He loves his peppermint socks, on which the fish-stick girl has complimented him.

He hates his reindeer socks, on which another human once vomited.

He draws a boy with a nose-shaped stomach.

He steers clear of medical students arguing the death drive in the cafeteria.

He is no longer allowed to operate his car.

He knows his roommate hates the president, and why.

He hears the improv troupe member say, If *they* don't laugh, nobody will.

He loves the fish-stick girl.

He does not love the fish sticks.

He smiles when she says, Nice socks, sailor.

He refused to let go until he could hear the choking man's lungs making breath.

He wets his eye with a wet napkin.

He is not stupid.

He is not a genius either.

He is not a bad driver either.

He is aware, yes, of why he is here.

He is here to be judged on the merits of his footwear.

He is aware that it would behoove him to take more seriously the seriousness of his situation.

He won't look the doctor in the eye, because the doctor has radiator eyes.

He looks him in the ear. Counts the lobe dents and hairs.

He may not be a genius, but he knows when fish meat has decayed.

He likes to pronounce *decayed* like *decade.*

He was for ten years frustrated, that old Odysseus!

He keeps *The Odyssey* on his nightstand so his roommate will fear him.

He draws the nose-bellied boy so his occupational-therapy counselor will fear him.

He diagnoses himself with milquetoastophobia: the fear of not making others afraid.

He asks to speak with the cafeteria supervisor.

He holds out half a grapefruit with a knife standing in it. This *pamplemousse,* he says, is older than my car.

He flinches when the supervisor takes a banana from the

steel bowl and draws his arm back, as if to fling.

He watches the improv troupers mince across the cafeteria like milquey meat until he *really* feels like killing himself.

He does not agree with the doctor that sketch comedy is a sassy little art form.

He hates to ask the doctor when he can go home and hear, You are in no way capable of meeting the demands of independent living.

He notices that *Hippocratic* is not too far from *hypocrite*.

He asks, What did the skull say to the electric-shock machine?

He answers, Thank you for not smoking.

He watches the doctor not be amused.

He thinks the doctor could use some swimming with dolphins.

He was for ten years minus one year a waiter of tables.

He does not wait any longer because of the lack of amusement people such as his doctor and the police feel about the saving of the choking man.

He thinks of the saving as angelic intervention when according to New York State law it was—

He *knows* angels aren't real, fuckwad!

He is sorry for saying that word.

He is sorry for letting saliva fly into the doctor's face.

He is not allowed, thanks to that word, into the TV room for two days.

He misses watching the human-misery shows.

He misses the other humans he watches the misery with.

He misses the restaurant where he waited until the day of the choking man.

He loves how the fish-stick girl has one curl that won't stay down.

He once wore socks with rifles on them, but she made no comment.

He misses her in the dark.

He feels for her in the dark.

He kicked in the groin the fuckwad who said that thing about her caboose.

He hates the word *caboose*.

He likes the word *groin*.

He was an English major at a good-in-many-people's-opinion college.

He cannot believe his doctor thinks the president of this country is doing a good job.

He wants a different doctor.

He read *The Odyssey* in college, so fuck you.

He will not get a different doctor.

He will not get in trouble for groin-kicking the fuckwad, because he bought his silence for ten dollars.

He recalls that the choking man was eating a ten-dollar plate of flesh.

He finds it stupid that news channels have been outlawed. Other types of misery are permissible—a man arrested for public dancing, a child born with turnips for hands, a contest called America's Most Resourceful Homeless Person—but war footage, says the doctor, loosens the patients' hinges.

He agrees with his roommate that hiding the bodies is an act of criminal obfuscation and that the doctor, like his Führer, would look good in handcuffs.

He likes how each color of candy in the TV room lives in its own dish.

He announces to the fish-stick girl, Human lung is a buttery meat.

He laughs when she blushes.

He adds, Whereas the heart tastes like pennies and the brains like raw lamb.

He diagnoses himself with sucrosintegrationophobia: the fear of candies mixing.

He hates when no red ones are left on account of the other humans hogged them.

He saw the choking poster every day at the restaurant, with its diagrams, instructions, beseechments. *Waste no time if this method fails.*

He thinks Penelope had eyes the color of go. Just like the fish-stick girl.

He is not so different, really, from Odysseus: both are sailors hunting for home.

I like the word *method.*

I dislike the word *buttery.*

I give the patients their three squares.

I have my favorites: the pigeon man, the periscope woman, the guy who intends to assassinate the president. And, of course, *him.*

I can't hold my breath for long.

I am thirty-one years old.

I have a big caboose that is admired by some.

I have one curl that won't stay down.

I diagnose myself with strapmouthophobia: the fear of not having much to say.

I tell him, Those are the best socks I've seen on you yet.

I watch him smile, and smile too. (There is something contagious.)

I can't stop talking about his footwear.

I blush when my supervisor says, No fraternizing with the lost minds.

I ask, Any new jokes today?

I lift a dollop of crushed potato above his tray.

I blush when he says, Your eyes are so green I forget all my jokes.

I mislaunch the potato, which blops onto the tray-runner and drips to the floor.

I laugh because he laughs.

I shiver through the rest of my shift.

I go home and run it like a tape: *Your eyes your eyes your eyes*.

I don't think his mind has been lost.

I suspect that when he yells at my supervisor, Stop feeding us cattle that died from the blackleg! he is making a veiled reference.

I don't think it's a person's fault if other people don't get his references.

I look skeptical when he claims he can hold his breath for three minutes. But secretly I believe him.

He tells the fish-stick girl, In ancient Rome, soldiers were paid in salt. Hence our word *salary*.

He wishes he could laugh when she says, Well *mine* is only a few grains! but it really wasn't funny.

He pretends to choke, gallantly diverting attention from her humor.

He coughs up one of the pennies he keeps at the back of his mouth and throws it (but not hard) at the supervisor and says, Get your money out of my lunch!

He misses how at the restaurant they'd fold slices of dog shit into the orders of rude customers, then happily watch the chewing mouths.

He leans up against the glass cough guard and whispers, Angels aren't real—I know that.

He is crying a little. (Though not in a crazy way.) I *know* you know! says the fish-stick girl.

He wonders what the mailman ever brings to the franzy house, other than socks and letters that notify: *Your life goes on without you.*

He has agreed to drive the getaway car for his roommate, provided they're both back on the surface while this president is still in office.

He squeezes his eyes when the medical student asks him how he likes it here.

He says, Where—in this cage? and the medical student says, So the hospital feels like a cage to you?

He says, It isn't a simile. Points at the window: barred. The other window: barred.

He senses the medical student's disappointment, so he throws him a little bone of crazy. Hearts of oak, he cries, did you go down alive into the homes of death?

He is impatient with the fish-stick girl.

He tried to tell her this morning how this place is its own magic mountain, where the hero arrives for a three-week vacation believing he is healthy and ends up staying seven years—but she didn't get it. She *pretended* to (smiles and nods) yet he saw the rockets in a line, unfired, wicks wet through.

The hero feels more at home, he added, in an Alpine sanatorium for lung complaints among the sick and nearly dead than in the so-called normal world! but she blinked in a way that reminded him of ocean arachnids who live so many fathoms down their eyes have no reason to grow.

He can't develop his theory with her, nor with the other humans in the TV room; and his roommate, though intelligent and reasonable, has little time for theories. Wants only to discuss methods of execution.

He draws the nose-bellied boy on a napkin during their nonoptional monthly dose of improv.

He waves it above his head.

He shouts at the troupers, Here comes one scurvy type leading another! God pairs them off together, every time. Swineherd, where are you taking your new pig, that stinking beggar there, licker of pots?

He won't stop until a nurse escorts him out of the cafeteria.

He wonders how the doctor can possibly think dinosaur-loose-in-supermarket or quiz-show-for-amnesiacs will lift a single spirit. If anything, these gags crush spirits like so many scuppernongs.

He likes how each grape of the arbor lives on its own tendril, and each tendril lives in its own follicle, and the fish-stick girl has a follicle that builds a wayward curl.

He rubs at night his own nipples, his own damp penis. His thumbs are her thumbs.

He hopes his roommate can't hear.

His breath is like a little train.

He thinks the lung must get its golden flavor from the shiny lies humans are perpetually inhaling.

He was only obeying the poster!

He thought the method was failing, so he wasted no time.

He was only saving a life.

He can't believe the doctor when he says the choking man wasn't choking.

He knows the doctor lies because the president, loved by the doctor, lies.

He diagnoses himself with dupophobia: the fear of being lied to by people stupider than you.

He saw the choking man clawing his throat. Universal sign for!

He dropped his plates and ran.

He hugged the man like a bear lover.

He made a fist under his heart.

He did not stop when the man said stop.

He did not stop when the man's girlfriend said stop.

He did not stop when another waiter said, Stop it, fuck-wad! and tried to wrench him off.

He could not stop until the life was saved.

I miss him the week he spends in the infirmary. (Pennies tore his bottom on their way out, according to the nurse's aide I paid ten dollars.)

I miss him a lot.

I have things to tell him, such as in ancient Greece there were temples where sick people slept in order to dream their own cures.

I have worked for three years at the franzy house, but the last three months have been the best by a landslide.

I was waiting for him.

I'm stupid, though, because how can you wait for a person you didn't know was coming?

I'm not stupid, but my mouth is strapped.

I read last night in a poem: *They did not meet, so they could never be parted.*

I want to lend him the book the poem's in.

I am suspicious of the new server on my shift—an eyelash-batter.

I hate people who say, Does my ass look ginormous in these pants? when they have asses the size of tennis balls.

I picture taking a pan of boiling water to her lashes.

I tell her, Why don't you take your fifteen? when he comes through the double doors, walking a little stiff. (What kind of socks today?)

I am so glad to see him.

I crane over the cough guard: sting rays.

I've never read *The Odyssey* but say, Oh totally! when he asks.

I'm sorry.

I stare helpfully at the next person in line but he says, What for? and I say, Nothing! and he insists, No, really, why are you sorry? and I say, Oh, just—I gave you the broken piece of pie.

I smile when he says, That's all right, I'm watching my figure.

I tell him that on my drive to work I pass a church whose sign says, EXPOSURE TO SON MAY PREVENT BURNING.

I ignore the next person in line.

I want him to answer wittily—take a jab at religious hypocrisy, or make up his own and better pun. But he says, Whales' backs don't burn when they breach because a vitreous oil secreted by their epithelium deflects ultraviolet rays.

I worry that institutional living is infecting him. With non sequiturs.

I ask, So where do you find all your various socks? and he answers, Mother sends.

I say, Oh.

I believe there are many ways to choke.

I don't think a blocked trachea is the worst of them.

I mean, yes, you'll die if your flesh-clogged windpipe is not poked clear, but is that actually worse than years of nothing to say?

I slither my fingers down at night, like they are his fingers.

I am a stealer.

I take snapshots of other people's heads.

I take their fingers and put them in my crotch.

I need to get him out of here.

I'm afraid he will turn into one long non sequitur if I don't.

I can borrow disguises from my sister's human-puppet college.

I'll drive so fast they can't catch us.

I am a good driver.

I'll give him my bed and take the couch. Unless he says, Hey, come here.

I drop a pan of lasagna from picturing it so hard.

I don't even mind when the lash-batter says, Oh my god, *loser!* because soon I will never see her again.

I will give him sugar cake for breakfast. Grapefruit so young it hurts your eyes.

I will take him for walks around my neighborhood, which has feral cats and a lightning-struck tree.

I will read aloud from a book of his choice.

I won't worry any more about my breath stopping in the night, because if it does, he will start it.

He nods while her mouth moves, but really, what is she saying?

He is smiling because she is.

He is thinking, What about the misery shows? (The other humans often need him on hand to explain plot and character while they suck themselves into sucrose trances.)

He likes the red best. But there is never enough.

He likes the green under Penelope's lashes.

He hates how worried she looks, so he keeps nodding.

He thinks, If any god has marked me out again for shipwreck, my tough heart can undergo it. What hardship have I not long since endured at sea, in battle! Let the trial come.

He says, All right, lamb, see you then.

He adds, I shrive thee of all blame for Tuesday's fungus-riddled cod.

•

I run it: *lamb lamb lamb lamb lamb.*

I know he'd never say it to the eyelash-batter. He doesn't even look at her, usually.

I repeat the word until my tongue hurts.

I am still holding the barrister wig, even though no one will be needing it.

I blink at the pink light growing on the floor.

I was clear, wasn't I, in naming midnight as our appointed time?

I diagnose myself with dawnophobia: the fear of dawn.

I bet he fell asleep by mistake.

I wonder if his roommate caught him on his way out. Informed the nurses' station.

I don't think the roommate would rat; he is not a fan of people in charge.

I hope he'll whisper apologies in the breakfast line. Raincheck on our rendezvous, lamb?

I won't be able to stand it if—instead—he looks at me in that I-am-not-actually-here way and mentions a sea creature.

I will, though.

I will stand it.

I dry my eyes with a dry napkin.

I go through a whole stack—ten times ten—of suggestion cards in their plastic bin, writing the same thing on every card: *Please cancel your contract with the improv comedians.*

HANDFASTING

When the stranger walks into the restaurant, I am still listening to Kasko talk dirty to my sister. I've been listening all morning and hating Kasko and hating my sister for putting up with it. She does more than put up. She leans across the marbled counter, between poached-egg orders, bends close to his big thick face and keeps her lips apart. The spit glitters in her mouth.

Sarah isn't spending many nights at home. She sleeps at Kasko's trashed apartment between his crusty sheets. My parents allow this because my sister is out of high school and earns her own money. I am thinking, when the stranger walks in, about drawing up a list of Kasko's crimes. My parents might be interested in seeing it.

Hello there, says the stranger to Sarah, and leans primly against a stool. His white shirt is stained blue from the fountain pens sticking out of its pocket. He orders hot water and dry toast and explains he is looking for witches. Yes, he says, it's a strange thing to look for, but we must understand, he is writing a dissertation about them.

Aren't any here, says Kasko. Town's full up on *bitches* however.

I'm not talking about the broomstick kind, says the stranger.

Witches are not just a matter of the seventeenth century. They are alive among us.

But not here, repeats Kasko. Look around you—there's *nothing* here.

There is a bank, a courthouse, a pharmacy. A green square where two streets meet. Around the corner is the Vietnamese café where Kasko rinses sauce off dishes and uses the long distance for booking bands that come to play at the VFW for the kids of Wolvercote, old kids, little kids, our hands full of beer.

My sister in her pink uniform with a tiny black star at either breast sets down the toast and hot water. The stranger dips one of the unbuttered triangles into the cup. Softens it, he murmurs.

She nods and asks, So what kind *are* they?

Modern-day witchcraft, he says, assumes many guises. You have your run-of-the-mill goth girl. Your senile herb-dicer. Your lesbian bookshop owner. Your California blood-guzzler. Your sober alcoholic in search of a new spirituality. And then there are—the renegades. They don't fit into a category because they're either insurgent or incompetent.

Kasko tells him he is barking up a blind alley. Sarah nods. Davey and the line cook nod.

I don't move my head.

You sure you got the right Wolvercote? says Kasko.

This is it, replies the stranger. There are no other Wolvercotes of interest to me.

How did the stranger know where to look? The witch wasn't here long. She passed through, is gone. Kasko says that whoever mentions her name gets a beating. He is full of big talk. But he can, if he wants to, break my bones. He tortures squirrels; he once shot a dog without remorse.

114

This stranger owns a very nice selection of pens, sleek and heavy, with slanting tips and drippy ink. He asks questions and writes down what the others say. I am the youngest and stay quiet. There aren't any grown-ups around except the mailman, reading his paper in the corner, and he is deaf. Sarah pours coffee and refills our waters and tongs crullers out of the glass case.

What does the word *Wicca* mean to you? asks the stranger.

My friend Flicka! shouts Davey from down the counter, where he and the line cook are playing two-handed spades.

The stranger persists. Have you heard this term before? Has anyone around here used the term?

We're very uneducated, sniffs Kasko. We don't use terms.

Sarah offers the stranger a cruller, but he says he can't handle sugar. I get bloated and lethargic, he explains. He touches very lightly the back of her hand that holds the green flowered plate. Kasko, noticing, says this interview needs to wrap up and what else does he want to know for God's sake?

So far you've told me *nothing* I want to know. You have described some customary social practices that include—he looks at his notes—the listening to of extremely marginal music, and the pushing over of cows as they stand in fields. You have intimated that nobody over the age of twelve in this town is a virgin.

He said virgin, yells Davey from the cards.

When the lunch rush starts, the stranger says he's off to the Red Roof Inn on the highway to write up his notes. We watch him go. Kasko announces his theory: the guy is on a hunt for tender meat. He has a thing for girls who wear black and use period blood in their potions. A fetish, he explains. This research is a front.

Sarah isn't persuaded. He doesn't look dirty, she says, just kind of pathetic.

Sex criminals, says Kasko, never look like sex criminals.

He was wearing a wedding ring, my sister points out. I didn't notice this; neither did Kasko. It's the sort of thing girls notice.

The witch's eyes were painted purple and black. Back in April, I looked straight into them and asked for a spell. Cut those two apart, was my request. She followed my pointing finger to Kasko and Sarah, entwined. I'll see what I can do, she said.

The stranger comes back the next morning. We are waiting. We would be waiting anyhow, because it's July, the heat is wet and terrible, and the Morning Star has central air. My parents' house does not have central air. The movie theater, two towns over, does not open until the afternoon.

He starts asking the same questions as the day before, and Kasko, Sarah, and Davey give the same answers. Nothing. Nope. Never noticed. The stranger is getting frustrated. Keeps asking the same things. Have we seen any girls collecting rainwater in bowls? Wearing milky stones on chains around their necks? Carrying a double-edged blade with runes carved into the handle?

Don't blame us for the no-witches situation, says Kasko. He's got a satisfied look I can't stand.

I say loudly, Why don't you talk to Egg Boy?

Shut up, Giles, they all go at once.

Who is Egg Boy?

A retarded person who lives under the town bridge, declares Kasko. Next question?

The stranger looks at me, hard. Giles, who is Egg Boy?

From across the table, Kasko is staring too. He shakes his head just the tiniest bit, and tucks his lips behind his teeth.

116

He lives under the bridge and steals eggs from neighboring farms, I answer reluctantly. But the stranger is writing it down. He seems excited. He finishes the coffee in his cup and slurps up what spilled into the green saucer. I look over his shoulder at the notebook and read *LOCATE EGG BOY* in big bleeding blue letters.

Egg Boy, whose heart was torn to pieces and left in the road, now keeps to himself in his apartment above the package store. His bad moods are feared and his grief is respected. People only discuss his plight in whispers, and never with grown-ups, much less strange ones. I'm actually not sure if this stranger is a grown-up or not. He dresses old—corduroy pants and white button-downs and thick brown shoes—but his face is soft and pimply. He doesn't seem much older than Kasko or the other boys who are already done with high school.

I leave the Morning Star while the stranger is still sitting there, before Kasko can hit or lecture me. I take my bike away from town into the meadows, the pine woods, hiding in the heat until supper.

Do your spells really work? I asked the witch. A bunch of us were having beers at the VFW, where the manager doesn't believe in underage drinking laws. If you're old enough to stop a bullet for the U.S. government, you're old enough to get blinkered, he says. I am not old enough to stop a bullet for the U.S. government, but I drink there anyway.

They work, she said vaguely. Destruction of love bond—it's a common rite. But it might take some time.

I wanted her to hurry, before my sister did something stupid like marry him.

On the third morning, the stranger doesn't come. We sit in the cool air stirring packets of sugar into burnt coffee. When

Kasko gets bored of telling my sister how hard he'll get up in her snatch, he informs me I'm a brainless baby bitch and if I don't learn to keep my mouth shut he will shut it permanently. Kasko never can come up with his own phrases. He just repeats what people say on cable. I wait for Sarah to defend me. After he calls me bitch a second time, she goes, Shut up, Kask, but in a dozy voice, not fierce at all. I sit there hating them both.

At noon Kasko leaves for his shift at the Vietnamese café. The Morning Star begins to crowd with grown-ups on lunch break from the bank, the pharmacy, the courthouse. I think of the stranger folding blue-stained shirts into a suitcase at the Red Roof, digesting his unsatisfying continental breakfast, driving his rental back to the airport. He will not find Egg Boy. The grown-ups of Wolvercote don't know any Egg Boy; they think his name is Earl.

Davey, I say, lemme borrow your truck for a minute.

How long is a minute?

Short. And I'm a good driver.

You are a good driver, he has to admit. Next year, when I take the learner's permit test, I will surely get a perfect score.

I find the stranger in the Red Roof parking lot, trash bag in hand, picking coffee cups and candy wrappers off his car seats. He is sweating like a hog.

I was worried you'd've checked out already.

Checked out? Hardly, he says. There is more to investigate. For instance, there's not a single bridge within a fifteen-mile radius of Wolvercote—hence, Egg Boy cannot live under one.

But he could still be retarded, I remind him.

Is he?

I look at the stranger's finger, the one with the ring. He's actually smart as hell, I say. He was in Sarah's class at school.

118

She said he wrote English papers that made you want to cry they were so beautiful.

And he, in his intelligence, might be familiar with witch-craft?

Well, maybe not so much the craft as the witch, I say.

The stranger flinches. Now we're getting somewhere.

She showed up last spring, I tell him, at the VFW with a band Kasko had booked at the last minute. They seemed to be big fans of death. Strips of white cotton wrapped tight around their bodies made them moving mummies. Plastic half-knives were Velcro'ed onto their chests and stomachs, trickling red thread. Their songs, which came out of a computer, sounded like people getting hit with violins and hammers. The girl sat at a table overseeing their tapes and stickers while they stood on stage pressing the buttons. Nobody bought any merchandise, but Egg Boy went over and made conversation. She was pissed-looking and pretty in her Egyptian makeup, her see-through net dress, her boots that climbed all the way up her thighs. Egg Boy was pissed-looking too.

The band left and she stayed. For a week the two of them holed up in his apartment above the packie. When they came down again, he told Kasko, his best friend since seventh grade, that he was going to marry her.

What name did she go by? asks the stranger. He seems like he might be about to throw up. His eyes are blinking very fast.

Are you really writing a paper on this?

What was her goddamn *name?*

Morrigan, I say.

The stranger nods, rubs his neck, stares down at the mottled Styrofoam in his hand.

So you're *not* writing a paper. Are you even in graduate school?

I am admiring the guy's ability not to cry when his eyes are so full of tears.

This Egg Boy, he says slowly, she was fucking him.

Well, they got married. What do you think.

He says nothing.

The majority of couples, I inform him, keep having sex regularly for at least the first three years of marriage.

Who told you that?

My sister. She read it in a magazine.

Did an actual ceremony occur? Was anyone *official* presiding? As in someone over the age of twenty-one?

No, but it was a real wedding. And they took their clothes off.

Lovely, he says, all cold.

The wedding was held at midnight in the back room of the Vietnamese café. Morrigan brought in a bunch of black lace and told me and Sarah to tack it up over all the windows. We didn't have any tacks so we used electrical tape. From the stereo came groaning organ music; from the rented dry-ice machine, fog that smelled like strawberries.

The kids gathered. Some of the older ones, Kasko's age, were about to turn into grown-ups; they had jobs and goatees and sometimes, by accident, babies. We stood around the room in our fanciest outfits. I wore my father's tuxedo pants and a sleeveless white T-shirt and a long black tie. My hair, stiff with Ivory, shot straight into the air. Sarah was in a vinyl dress that crammed her breasts up, and I tried not to look at them.

Kasko was the priest. He waited under the exit sign, which Morrigan had hidden with a wreath of plastic orchids, in the three-piece suit he wore to his mother's funeral last year. I was thinking he should have worn a cape instead, something not so Christian-looking, but Sarah explained that the suit brought him closer to the Dark Side, where his mother was, and thereby invested him with the powers necessary to preside over the ritual.

Morrigan and Egg Boy came out of the kitchen in bathrobes. Morrigan's midnight-blue hair was tied into clumps with little rubber snakes, and her eyes were painted in the shape of Cleopatra's. Egg Boy looked like he normally did—bald, angry—except for the bathrobe. They stood in front of Kasko and everybody got quiet.

Why are they wearing bathrobes? I whispered to Sarah.

Because they're doing the ceremony skyclad, she answered.

The robes dropped, making terrycloth pools at the feet of the bride and groom. I blinked at the sudden flesh. Morrigan had pointy shoulders and pimples on her back but her butt was plenty—I mean it was beautiful—round, soft, tilted up. I stared at its surging, the high curving slice, the two dents at the bottom of her spine. Her little pale legs were shaking. I pictured my hands on her waist, lightly clamped. I kept my eyes away from Egg Boy, afraid of seeing what a handsome guy's butt looked like. I was sure it would not resemble mine.

I could not see their fronts but Kasko's stupid lizard eyes crawled down, looking at what he shouldn't. He saw it on my sister—wasn't that enough? He stared until Egg Boy kicked his suited leg.

Consulting the script Morrigan had written out for him, Kasko bellowed, There are those in our midst who seek the bond of handfasting. Let them be named and brought forward.

Morrigan and Egg Boy each took a tiny step, but there was not much room to go before they hit Kasko.

Are you Gwyll? said Kasko.

I am, said Egg Boy. (Morrigan had told him he needed a name more appropriate to the ceremony.)

What is your desire?

Egg Boy looked down at his arm, where he had written out his part. To be made one with Morrigan in the eyes of the gods and the Wicca.

Kasko said to Morrigan, Are you Morrigan?

I am.

And what is your desire?

To be made one with Gwyll in the eyes of the gods and the Wicca.

After taking one more glance at her tits, Kasko reached behind him for the plastic sword that had been borrowed from Davey's uncle, who did seasonal work at the Delaware Historical Society acting out the Revolutionary War. He raised up the sword then handed it to Morrigan and Egg Boy, who grasped it between them.

Here before you, boomed Kasko, stand two of your folk. Witness, now, that which they have to declare.

In my version for the stranger, I don't mention looking at their butts. I don't tell about seeing Kasko, after the whiskey toasts, put a finger on my sister's nose and softly say, What about a handfasting for *us?* Sarah laughed and shook her head so his finger slipped off. Not for us, she said.

Let's get in the car, Giles, says the stranger. This heat's not fit for man or beast. We climb in and he turns the key; the air conditioning comes blasting. His eyes are wet but they still aren't dripping. I wait for him to say something. What he says finally is, I'm John. We haven't been properly introduced.

Can I smoke in this car?

You may. The ceremony you describe is a Wiccan marriage rite. I've come across it in my research.

What's the research for, if you're not writing anything?

The bride, he goes on, happens to be someone quite, that is to say extremely, dear to me. Her name is Abby.

From his shirt pocket he takes a postcard, creased and soft. It is a picture of the Wolvercote courthouse in the fall, with leaves piled red on the square. On the back there is only one sentence: *Everything in this town reminds me of falling down.*

How do you know she wrote it? I ask.

It's in her hand. She has a very accomplished, a very graceful hand.

The letters are spidery, slanted, curled—the writing of a person who wants people to think she is mysterious.

He gets something else out of his pocket. It's a photograph of a girl standing on a lawn in a light green thin-strapped dress with yellow flowers stamped all over it. She seems embarrassed and is not smiling. This girl looks like your average girl, maybe a little prettier than your average girl. Her hair is dark blonde. Her lipstick is pink. If this is Morrigan, she's deep undercover.

That's her? She looks all normal and shit.

This is her—*before,* says John. I ask before what, and he says before she got the idea in her head that college and hamburgers and having sex in the missionary position were going to extinguish her soul. And this was her sunsuit, he says, that I bought for her two summers ago. She called it a dress, but it was more of a sunsuit.

She definitely wasn't wearing *that* when she came to Wolvercote.

I imagine not. She burned it shortly before she left me. I got home from class one night and she had this little bonfire going in the kitchen sink. The sunsuit was in flames; so was

the phone bill, a letter from her mother, and our marriage cer-
tificate.

That sucks, I say.

Her witch phase had been going on for a few months by
that time. The books and herbs and amulets—but mostly the
new wardrobe. She jacked hell out of our credit card. Started
doing a kind of Halloween-on-the-banks-of-the-Nile makeup
routine. Made a witchy friend at the New Age bookstore. She
thought about joining a coven, but the nearest one was a ninety-
minute drive.

She needed a change, I conclude.

John taps a pen against his lips and says, What confuses me
is why your fellow members of the rural underground are so
secretive about her having been here. Is it from boredom? The
need to build drama where there is actually rather little?

Kasko is his best friend, I explain. He won't let him be dis-
graced any further. He says Morrigan was a fatal gash in the
vein of Egg Boy's manhood.

The vein of his manhood?

The chick made a fool of him. It amounts to a castration.

So says Kasko?

I shrug. I don't like talking about Kasko. His name brings
up pictures of Sarah without any clothes on, eyes shut, writhing
on a gritty sheet and making noises like the girls on the videos
Davey keeps in a cooler in his parents' garage. But I want John
to understand his terribleness. Did you know he tortures squirrels? I say. He rigs traps where they strangle slowly until he lets
them go. They make horrible little coughing sounds, after. And
he shot a dog once in the foot and bragged about it. And his
name sounds like a gas station.

That's awful, says John, but he isn't paying attention. Will
you take me to see him?

Who?

Humpty Dumpty. He of the manly vein.

He's not really into visitors, I mumble. But okay.

After the witch agreed to cast a spell for me, I looked hard for evidence of success. If my sister slept at home for two nights running, I thought Morrigan had triumphed. If I detected a grain of irritation in Sarah's throat when she said Kasko's name, I silently congratulated the Dark Side. But nothing, really, when it came down to it, was changing. I still caught them kissing behind the counter when I stopped at the Morning Star after school. I still heard him whisper, in public earshot, about sticking it in her.

I went by the apartment above the packie. I wanted to ask her why the spell wasn't working. She might need different herbs, or a frog to grind up. (I would offer to catch one.) In the stairwell I heard screaming.

What're you talking about? What the fucking *fuck* are you talking about?

HOW CAN YOU BE SO MORONIC YOU DON'T KNOW WHAT I'M TALKING ABOUT?

I waited on the landing until the screaming stopped. It stopped and I kept waiting and then Morrigan came gunning out the door, black dress afloat. Oh, she said, it's you! but did not stop. I followed her down two flights into the bright wash of beer light.

Can you please do that spell again? I said. It's not working that great.

What? Fuck, I have no cigarettes.

Here. I held out my pack. The antilove spell, remember? For my sister and the asshole.

She filled her chest with smoke and said, Look.

With that one word, I understood.

I'm sorry, she said. I'm just not a very good witch.

You're a *fake* witch, I corrected.

Morrigan glared back at me, then turned to squint up the block. There was nothing to see. Will you get your parents' car, she said, and take me to the nearest train?

On the highway, John drives slowly and keeps readjusting the rearview mirror. Davey is going to be mad that I abandoned his truck at the Red Roof. But I'm not afraid of Davey. He's too little to break anyone's bones.

She was a waitress, says John, as if answering a question, at the diner down the street from my apartment. I had breakfast there twice weekly before my sociology class. I was very shy. You've seen her, so you understand my reasons for shyness. She noticed my books on the table. She was in college too, a psych major. She had never heard Brazilian music. I took her to hear it.

This is before she got all dark and shit?

He nods. This is when her favorite meal was cole slaw and hamburgers. When she enjoyed her sitcoms.

And when you were fucking her, I add, relishing the chance to say this word without lowering my voice.

John snaps, I would really appreciate your not talking like that about my wife.

But you said—

Stop it! His upper lip is twitching. Red spots jump in his cheeks. Have some goddamn respect.

Sorry, I say, and I am. He is doing pretty poorly, this John. He does not seem well. His face has the same quivery, fish-skinned look my mother's gets right before she refills her prescription.

He parks in front of the neon beer signs. Two floors up, we

stop at a door hung with a huge poster for a band Kasko has been trying to book for years but who are too good to come here. The ones who come have no place better to play. John looks disapprovingly at the screaming corpse on the door, its bony hands raised in pleading.

Egg Boy opens at our knock. He is shirtless, in black sweatpants, and obviously hasn't bothered to shave his head in several days. Soft shoots of gold are growing in. His chest, which I've always envied for its hardness, does not look so hard. The belly swells out from under the ribs.

Giles, he nods.

Can we come in for a second?

Egg Boy shrugs, stands back. The room, painted a dark streaky red, with black plastic sheets tacked over the windows, smells like toe lint. The only places to sit are bed and floor; we all stand.

How you been keeping? asks Egg Boy.

Fine, I say, and look at John, because I can't think of a way to introduce the topic. The smell in the room is making me breathe through my mouth.

John, says John and reaches to shake Egg Boy's hand. I'd like, if I may, to ask you about Morrigan.

Egg Boy sticks out his chin. I remember how he clocked a boy once in the grocery store parking lot, a clean quick smash, and the boy didn't get up for half an hour. That little cunt? What about her?

John coughs. She's my wife.

She's *my* wife. My cunty wife.

I think of my bike leaned up against a bench on the square, under the maples, where I left it this morning. I want to be on it, riding. I want not to see the skin under Egg Boy's eyes sagging weirdly.

Are you the college motherfucker she used to live with? She told me about you. I pictured you with little granny glasses.

John reaches to dab sweat off the sides of his nose. She didn't tell you we were married?

Uh, *no*.

Ah, says John. He sounds very tired. She left me in February, and I've been looking for her. I just want to know what happened. I want to tell her she can always come back.

The coming-back part changes Egg Boy's face. A shudder unclenches his jaw. You would take her? he says. After she dicked you so royally?

I can't hate her. I've tried. I can't.

It's easy, says Egg Boy. Just think of how she put her head on your stomach at night and said *This is so much better than anything* and how she talked about the kids you'd have, how you would dress those kids in tiny black boots and the kids would have your sexy blue eyes. Think of how she said *We'll go to Scotland where they have castles*. Think of how pretty she was.

She was pretty, agrees John.

Egg Boy sits down on the bed. John kneels to the floor, leans back against the minifridge. I feel stupid standing. I'm gonna take off, I say.

You mind running by the Star to get us some sandwiches? says Egg Boy. Tell your sister to put them on my tab. Turkey club, no lettuce.

Ham and swiss, please, says John. I notice he has quit sweating.

The lunch rush is over and Sarah is reading the newspaper. The line cook sits smoking. Davey isn't around.

Can you make me a couple of sandwiches?

You going on a picnic? she asks.

It's for me and the guy doing witch research.

I thought he left town.

Nope, he remains. Turkey club, no lettuce, and a ham and swiss.

She gives the order to the line cook, who nods but stays where he is, smoking.

You be home for supper tonight? I ask. They're showing vampire-bite survival stories on the sci-fi channel.

I don't think so, she says. I have to meet up—

—With him after his shift. I know. What, are you guys *engaged* or something? He tortures squirrels.

He does not.

Oh yes he damn does. I saw him. And he shot that dog in the leg.

Which was an accident. Look, baby bear, we'll watch a movie tomorrow night. We can rent if there's nothing good on. And I'm not engaged. Most definitely *not* engaged.

But I see them on the sheets, his huge body pressing the air out of her small one, sauce and dirt from under his fingernails smeared across her stomach. I hear him making fast high grunts like the gigantically hung actors on Davey's videos. Lunging, stabbing, shoveling, so rough she starts to cry. She is crying and then it's not Kasko on her, it's John, skinnier and frecklier, but he holds her wrists against the wall so she can't leave. *Let me go,* my sister whispers. *I am late for supper.*

She asks do I want any chips. I shake my head and Sarah goes back to reading the paper. It's a long time before the line cook gets up to make the sandwiches. In the wait, I try to clean the pictures out. I want my head empty of bodies on beds, of stabbing bodies, of Kasko's voice telling my sister he's going to lick his fingers and slide them up her gash until she begs.

•

Back at Egg Boy's, the husbands are drinking from plastic cups illustrated with the planet Jupiter and their faces have gotten redder. A record is playing of a guy singing sadly in French. I lay the wrapped sandwiches in the middle of the floor.

Think of how, says John, she dumped her nonpareils into her popcorn at the movies, because chocolate and corn are delicious together.

We never went to the movies, says Egg Boy, but think of how she threw you up against the sink in the BK men's room and took off your belt and wrapped it around your neck and put the buckle in her mouth before she—

Think of how ticklish she was at the backs of her knees.

How sweet she looked in crotchless panties.

John helps himself from the bottle of brown liquor on the floor. No, how sweet she looked in her *sunsuit,* standing in our backyard. It was my job to mow the grass.

Hit me up, says Egg Boy, holding out his cup. John pours. Egg Boy turns to me, blinks his sagging eyes. Love is a joke, he announces.

Indeed, says John. A farce. A *folly.*

Yeah? I say.

Show him the thing, suggests John.

Egg Boy reaches under the bed and takes out a postcard with an aerial view of adobe houses clustered on red sand. It's postmarked Proctor, Arizona. One sentence only. *Travel keeps me from falling down.*

She just goes along her merry way, shouts John. His voice knocks against the walls of the tiny room.

When I pulled up in front of the train station, the witch asked for one more cigarette. We smoked softly in the dark. I did try, you know, she said. I looked it up in my book. I spoke the incantations. I put water and fire in every corner of the room.

Maybe your book is fake?

She scratched her cheek and said, It was written by an expert practitioner.

Which train are you taking? I asked.

The first one that comes, said Morrigan. It was the kind of thing the characters would say in the 1950s road-trip novel we read last spring for English. All the kids in my class loved that book. A few of them even said they were going to quit school and hop trains. But nobody did.

Good luck, I told her.

Thanks. And by the way—don't worry. Your sister will make it out of here soon enough.

John is waving the bottle at me. Giles, partake with us!

Yeah man, says Egg Boy, you need some practice. Want a cup?

No thank you, I say.

Straight from the jug, then!

No thank you.

My bike is still chained to the bench. I want to be riding. These boys have clamped their hands at a girl's waist, felt her heels on their spines. But they are just sitting here now. The girl has gone. Until today I felt guilty for helping her go, angry her spell didn't work. Now I'm looking at the boys she left and seeing the boy my sister will leave. I am wanting her away from the green square and pink uniform and scabby sheets under wriggling skin. I am wanting her on trains, with me.

BLOTILLA TAKES THE CAKE

At our morning session, Linda says I have to tell about the birthday party. I can't keep putting it off. You've been here for weeks, she reminds me. It's time to unload your shame.

It was just a dumb thing that happened a long time ago.

And where did it ultimately lead? she asks. Where did you end up as a result?

St. Petersburg, Florida . . . ?

I want to give the right answer. I wait for a hint. She just stares back. Her gold bangle earrings faintly sway. Finally she checks her watch. And why did you come here to St. Petersburg?

I got sick.

You were bleeding from your rectum, she corrects. And that is not a normal state of affairs.

At Palm Terrace, a bloody ass isn't really such a big deal. They've seen worse: women too big to get onto the toilet by themselves—women wearing diapers because they've permanently lost control of their bowels—nineteen-year-old girls falling over cold from heart attacks.

I'm not so bad, you see.

Take my roommate, Viv. She got her stomach stapled a year ago but the operation didn't do any good. Though her stomach is the size of a bean, she remains a hundred pounds overweight. Milkshakes, she explains, and whatever else you feel like mashing up in a blender.

Viv has lost hope. All this, she'll say, with a sweep of her hand across our neatly made beds and flower vase on the dresser, is it going to change anything? In group, she sits shaking her head—she doesn't think it will work, the talking, the crying, the hugs and affection. Back in Cincinnati, where her equally skeptical husband is waiting, this place will seem like a goopy dream.

We don't have to keep eating like that anymore, I remind her sternly.

Yeah, she says, but we're probably going to anyway.

After my session with Linda, it is time for lunch. Our group slouches toward the battlefield: skeletons in wheelchairs, circus fat ladies, green-skinned girls. Bringing up the rear is Linda, festive in her lavender sari.

One of the skeletons says, My stomach hurts. I should be resting.

Linda shushes her and we continue, at glacial speed.

The dining room has pink walls, blue carpet, and plastic palm fronds in every corner. The rehab patients are still in line, running behind schedule. They eat twenty minutes earlier because they get different food from ours, regular things like fried chicken and macaroni. After they go through, the cooks clear away all the good stuff and bring out our specialty items. The turkey loaf, the flax seed.

The junkies are taking their good sweet time today, says Murphy at my shoulder, though not maliciously. She is just hungry. I understand. I am hungry too, but I remember what my mother used to tell me: Hunger is only a state of mind. A feeling, not a fact.

More goddamn potatoes, please! yells Jerome. I know his name because his group often sings it when he gets up to clear his tray at the end of a meal: *Jerome, Jerome, baby Jerome, time to clean up, get your ass home.* Maybe singing is part of their therapy. On our unit, we do not sing.

The head cook dumps another scoop onto Jerome's plate and frowns down the line at the mesmerized overeaters, whose eyes are locked on the hamburger buns.

It's not fair that we have to *see* that, whispers Sandra. It's really rather sadistic.

When the warming dishes are replaced, we groan at the roughy with lemon, brown rice, rubbery stems of broccoli. One by one we hand the cook our meal cards. Each of us gets a different amount of food, depending on weight and preferred crime.

How goes it, Rachel? says the cook. Glad to be getting out soon?

I smile dutifully. The cook is a busy man; I don't need to bother him with the news that leaving Palm Terrace makes me sick to think about. Why would a person want to stay in a place where you're not allowed a single drop of coffee, where you're forced to put on a bathing suit for water aerobics? But I could stay forever.

At the end of the counter are little baskets of salt, pepper, and Sweet 'N Low. Linda watches to make sure we don't take more than one packet of each. Sweet 'N Low is a prized commodity, hoarded by anorexics to trade with overeaters for cigarettes or favors. Sandra, who's got a violent sweet tooth, has been known to pay cash. Charlotte, who is a bitch, charges a dollar per packet. Murphy, who has a heart of gold, gives Sandra her Sweet 'N Lows for free.

Much raucous laughter and spoon-clattering from the

rehab tables, but our corner of the dining room is loaded with silence. Eating, for us, is not a happy business. The overeaters struggle not to finish too fast. The anorexics fight to swallow. I mash everything up into one big pudding and my throat keeps closing at the thought of telling them about the birthday party, seeing their disgusted faces.

Not happening today, says Murphy, just not happening today. She stares at her untouched tray. She's wearing a sweatshirt so big it practically hides her from view. She is nothing but pink fleece and wet brown deer eyes. At forty-one she looks like a weather-beaten child.

Come on and hurry it the fuck up, says Charlotte. Her tray is clean, she has obediently shaken out her napkin for Linda's inspection, but I know her tactics. She drops food on the carpet, morsel by morsel, and grinds it under the heel of her sandal.

It won't digest, whispers Murphy. It's just going to sit there in my stomach, not digesting.

You've got to eat it anyway, says Linda.

But it'll just *sit* there!

No one can leave until every plate is empty. We all watch Murphy contemplate the sweating mounds of fish and rice.

Take a *tiny* bite, urges Sandra. You can do it, honey.

I can't I can't I can't. I'm sorry—Her big eyes well up, fluttering. I'm letting everyone down.

Just shove the shit in your mouth so we can get out of here! barks Charlotte. I want to lie out.

Sandra tells her, Your suntan is not important to us.

Settle down, says Linda. Murphy, you can do this. I know you think your stomach hurts, but it will actually feel much better once there's some nourishment inside.

I'm not making it up, whimpers Murphy. I don't just *think* it hurts, it *does* hurt!

I guess it's Ensure for you, then, madam.

The anorexics live in fear of Ensure. Sometimes they spit it out onto the table or floor, and scream when a second can is brought.

We'll get you the strawberry flavor, okay?

It's not okay, mumbles Murphy as Linda rolls her chair out from the table. It's very much not, not at all, okay.

We huddle around the wheelchair, carefully patting her shoulders. You can feel the bones right there under the skin, no padding whatsoever. It must be painful for skeletons like her to have sex. If they do have sex. Charlotte has it, or claims to, with the welder from her father's construction company to whom she's secretly engaged. As for Murphy, I'm pretty sure she does it with girls—or *did,* before she got so sick. It's just an instinct; she's never said anything. Sandra once asked her why she wasn't married, and Murphy said she didn't think the right guy was ever going to come along.

Back on our unit, while they're fixing up the Ensure, I inform Murphy that group is going to be boring this afternoon.

But it's always boring.

Extra boring. Linda says I have to tell some things.

Juicy things?

No.

There has been no juice in my life, only mistakes and lack of willpower. Murphy, on the other hand, has stories that would fill up weeks of television movies. She stopped eating not to stay thin but because being full reminds her of being pregnant. She has had two abortions, both on account of her father, who had sex with her for five years until she was removed to foster care. She doesn't mention it in group, but she tells me things out at the smoking table, under the umbrella, on the hot slow afternoons when we sit and smoke and stare at the palm trees. She talks about her father with businesslike eyes. That's so sad, I always whisper, and she nods, lighting another, It was sad, yeah, as if remembering a film she saw last year.

No matter what, I promise not to fall asleep, she says, adding shyly, I'm sure it will be good.

Murphy is a big reason I don't want to leave Palm Terrace. We smoke together. We make fun of the cook's hairnet. We stare discreetly at new arrivals on the rehab unit and, if there's a cute one like Jerome, Murphy will lie through her teeth and say he's looking at me.

I'm telling you, she shouts at the head nurse, I can't drink it. It's going to clog up my system. You want me to die from blockage?

Murphy has never shouted before. Everyone stops talking and looks. Linda and the nurse loom over her.

This can is not going to make you fat, bellows the nurse. Your body needs these nutrients.

I'll eat at dinner, begs Murphy. Just give me some time to digest breakfast.

You know the rules.

Fuck the rules, I know my own *stomach,* thank you very much!

It's strange to hear a vicious voice coming from that wilted little face.

Linda holds the can to her lips and Murphy smacks it away and off it flies, into the wall, pink rain splattering the linoleum. Murphy closes her eyes. She looks weirdly like the painting of Joan of Arc that hung in the hospital I went to, for evaluation, after the birthday party.

At one-fifteen we start group with our usual check-in around the circle. Charlotte complains about having to sit in a wheelchair to and from meals when her legs work just fine, and by the way her parents aren't paying millions of dollars for her to lose all her muscle tone. Viv passes. Sandra has just received a letter from her husband threatening divorce if she doesn't lose enough weight at Palm Terrace.

Is he aware that Palm Terrace is not a diet farm? asks Linda.

Oh, he's *aware,* all right.

Her husband is the Ice Cream King of St. Cloud, Minnesota, with five stores and wholesale distribution to supermarkets. Which I guess makes Sandra the Ice Cream Queen. She loves her husband but he refuses to sleep with her, even touch her, because she is a *flappy-cunted heifer.*

My husband would never say such a thing, declares Grace.

Only because he never talks to you. Sandra pats her gold-and-purple sundress across the twin mountains of her thighs.

Grace is a cutter. She takes razors to the rinds of her feet and hacks away, hobbling herself. She also gnaws off the tips of her fingers and is obliged to wear mittens. It is funny to see a mittened lady in this ninety-five-degree humidity, but Grace herself has no sense of humor about it. Instead, she is a tragic figure, the victim of a courteous but indifferent husband and a promiscuous daughter. Today she's obsessed about her daughter catching AIDS. She knows it would kill me, moans Grace, and she's ornery enough to risk it.

She's the one that would die, not you, points out Charlotte.

I will die first, of dread and humiliation. She is a common slut.

I've seen pictures of her daughter, a round-cheeked teen, smiling (though how could you smile, with a mother like that?), and not slutty-seeming at all.

Maybe you should pick something else to worry about, suggests Linda. For instance, your own health.

Grace sucks on her mittens, rolls her eyes. Somebody, I think, should prescribe her some new medication.

Linda checks her watch. Karen? Any thoughts?

Karen, a puker, is spacing out in the corner. Her neck is still swollen, cheeks puffy—she's only been here a couple of days—and from what I can tell, she's not the brightest bulb in the chandelier. What? I'm sorry, what?

How are you doing today?

I'm good. Pass!

I'm the only one left, because Murphy is out fighting with the nurse. Linda's eyebrows shoot up in warning.

I begin in my book-report voice: When I was twelve there were some girls that lived on my street, and we all sort of hung out together. . . .

And I was the only chubby one. The others were blonde, but my hair was dark. Those girls played games like Race Down the Block. Amy Danbury always won. I never raced. I didn't see the point of, number one, losing, and number two, making my heart feel like it was going to split wide open.

It was Amy who chose my nickname. Your stomach, she said, is as big as my father's after he eats too much and needs to sit quietly because he's bloated. You're bloated all the time. You are . . . *Blotilla!*

The others cheered when she said that, Yes, that's so good—Blotilla! and I thought *That's stupid* but my mouth said nothing. My face was too hot for speaking. I was floating above them, above Amy in her size-small sweater, gliding off. I was glad my mother wasn't around at that moment to feel ashamed. My mother didn't need the aggravation. It was a very stressful time for her, thanks to my father, who had just moved to Montreal with a flight attendant and by doing so turned, said my mother, into a walking cliché.

Amy came up with other stupid ideas, like taking our measurements. She had bought a new tape measure and told us to pull up our shirts. Just to check, she said with a knowing smile. We'll write them down in my notebook.

I don't see any point in *that,* I said.

Are you scared, Blotilla?

What would I be scared of?

That the tape won't reach around your stomach?

Everyone laughed, of course, because when Amy said jump they said how high. I walked away before they could measure anything.

After that I avoided the girls, but our town was small. I saw them at school. I heard my new name in whispers, snorts, giggles—Blotilla, Blohhh-*tilla!* I was eating like a champ, and as I got bigger, my mother got smaller. What if she grew so thin she couldn't get out of bed, couldn't go to work, and I'd have to drop out of school and waitress at Applebee's to save our house?

I worked at Applebee's once, interrupts Karen.

I narrow my eyes; she is breaking the flow. Well, I didn't end up doing that, I say loudly, but I wanted to, because it would've given the lawyer some ammunition for the child-support case. My father would start writing checks *or else.*

And it wouldn't have been that bad, I figured at the time, never to go to school again. My mother would be so impressed by my work ethic that she would raise herself up on her elbows and ask for a plate of food. Her strength would return; she would fill out to her regular self. With her sleeping so much and being in a terrible mood, I didn't let her know about my tormenters. I didn't tell her who was calling in the evenings to say, May I speak to Blotilla? and hanging up when my mother told them wrong number.

When the invitation came for Amy Danbury's birthday, I couldn't explain why I didn't want to attend. All the parents on the block were invited too. But you don't have to go if you're not feeling up to it, I reminded my mother.

She said she might as well, since Gloria Danbury would be offended by her absence and it wasn't worth the aggravation.

So there was this party, I tell the group, and Amy had a humongous white coconut cake, and. . . . I pause, twisting my hands. The clock on the wall buzzes and clicks. Aren't we pretty much out of time?

Go on, Rachel, says Linda. What happened when they served the cake?

It was just a stupid thing.

Let the other women share it with you.

Everyone's eyes on me, even Karen's, even Viv's, and she normally falls asleep halfway through. Well, they started to cut the cake, Amy was serving it, we all had our little plates and were holding them out. . . .

And Amy delivered a slice to each plate, smiling like a princess, with the mothers standing around the table cooing and applauding. My mother had her fake-pleasant face on. When she got to me, Amy hesitated, then shook her head.

Rachel is watching what she eats, she announced.

There was a tiny silence, then Gloria Danbury whispered, Move on to the next one.

Please can I have a piece? I said politely. Amy looked at me with gloating pity and I added, in a smaller voice, Because it's a special occasion.

Amy said, I don't think you can afford these calories.

The other girls laughed.

My mother was blushing. *Blushing*. That little fuckface small-sweatered whore had embarrassed my mother.

I don't remember much after that, only the sun sparking off the knife in Amy's cute little hand, my ears ringing like the ocean. There was a lot of blood and it got all over the white cake. People were screaming but they sounded far away. The next place I went was the hospital, for evaluation.

Hold on! cries Sandra. What *happened?* Did you cut her?

Stab. I stabbed. I stabbed her and it severed tendons and she can never play piano with that hand again.

Like a wave breaking, they start to clap. Viv hoots and Grace whistles and even Charlotte nods approvingly.

Way to fucking go! yells Sandra. A stab for justice.

I wish Murphy were here. I think she would be proud of me too.

It is time for water aerobics. As we file out of the group room they all come up and hug me, even Viv, who is not a fan of hugs. They say she got what she deserved. They say it's good what I did. Deep down, I know that's not true. But what I love is that they don't care, the women here. They don't think I am a sociopath and are not bothered by the fact that for years I swallowed so many laxatives it made me bleed from my rectum.

I look for Linda so she can tell me I did a nice job. She is talking to the nurse. They are both frowning.

Where's Murphy? I ask. It is time to put on bathing suits and fill the pool with our various bodies, the big and the small and the medium, to flap our arms to the beat of early-eighties dance remixes and hear the overeaters complain their lungs are exploding.

Murphy has been discharged, says Linda.

The nurse pads off down the hall.

Charlotte says matter-of-factly, But she'll die.

We picture Murphy going back to her apartment across the bay in Tampa, where the refrigerator has not a single thing in it, where there is nobody to roll her around in a wheelchair so she can save her strength—Murphy who believes her stomach can't digest anything but cigarettes and diet Sprite.

Linda, who is paid to console us, says, Yes, I think she probably will.

I'm sorry, I say to nobody in particular.

You're banishing her, demands Sandra, for not drinking a can of liquid dog food?

It was more than just the Ensure, says Linda, adjusting the folds of her sari. Go get your suits on.

But, we say.

In the pool, we are lethargic. The aerobics instructor shouts louder and louder. I lie kicking on my back. The sky is ruthless, a brilliant blue that will go on being blue even after Murphy's heart stalls and her lungs cave in and her wrinkled kid's body drops to the linoleum with the same thud as a bag of groceries. My own body feels heavier than it ever has, like if I don't keep moving I will sink straight to my watery grave.

LEOPARD ARMS

A new family is taking the place of the woman who choked on a peanut. They arrive in a dented sedan. Their belongings are few. No lamps or saucepans, two chairs only, clothes in plastic bags. It's drizzling, so they hurry.

The little girl says, Who's that? and points up at me.

Nobody, says the no-haired mother.

Step lively, morsel! adds the rope-haired father.

My name is not a word; it's a smell. Call me the tang between smoke and scraped bark. Some years ago I fell to Brooklyn, was born as ornament on a block of cheap flats. The man who cut me was jolly and slapdash. His chisel was dull. He made my mouth open as if to growl, snout broad, eyes lashless. I wish I were more frightening. My shoulders, for one, are tiny—they barely protrude from the battlement—and my lips could as easily be laughing as scowling. I look as if I'd been carved with blunt scissors, by an only slightly talented child.

The word you know me by is from *gargouille,* the French for throat. A throat can sing a tune, swallow milk, be sliced wide open. Down throats go slender needles aimed at human hearts.

•

The family ensconced: parents pouring drinks, girl pacing along each new wall to listen.

A large red charabanc chugs past, its upper-deck riders ponchoed against the rain.

And here on our right, trumpets the guide, we have the apartment where Mel Villiers wrote *Still Life with Gaping Wound*. He waves his microphone at the stack of microlofts (formerly a public library) across the street. In the very same building, he continues, is where Polychrest recorded the eight-track demos of *Mumcunt*.

A gust of oohs from the deck.

When're we gonna see where Squinch Babbington's girlfriend overdosed? shouts a passenger. That was in the brochure.

Next block, says the guide.

If Mrs. Megrim had been on her lookout when the bus came by, those tourists would have gotten an earful. *Quit nosing, you nostrils! Why don't you go look at something actually interesting?* Megrim's husband is long dead, her children far flung. She sits on a plastic lawn chair outside the mouth of the building, condemning all who pass.

But today the only person who noticed the bus was the watcher, a young woman on the top floor who stays behind planked-over windows and touches the world through binoculars.

I watch too: the light dies. Dark water falls. The drinkers and dancers swim out. O kiss me please, o throw me over. Hot rooms stink, are entered and fled. With each small hour the frenzy hardens: *which of these fuckers can I bring back to bed?* Then the night unclenches. Birds' wings begin to itch, stumblershome pull keys from pants, and the old—already restless—wait on mentholated pillows until an acceptable hour to open their eyes. The sun staggers forth. There is only so much it can do, since along these narrow streets the buildings loom and tilt, keeping sidewalks in constant shade.

The edifice I grow from, five stories of blond stone, is called Leopard Arms. Its dwellers believe I am here to spout rain and to guard them. They're unaware I would make a fine witness for criminal trials. A gargoyle's ears collect sounds from impossible distances, and we don't need eyes to see. A mere adornment, a forgettable decoration, I know everything they do. But they don't do much. They are, in fact, a disappointing lot. I've heard tell of unpleasant posts—the church whose cleric drives tent pegs into the necks of prairie dogs, or the planetarium whose female staff drink one another's menstrual yield—so I suppose I ought to be grateful; but Leopard Arms is not the most electrifying assignment in Brooklyn. Many of its residents rarely leave the premises. The ones who do don't get far; they return an hour later, bag of provisions on an arm, looking exhausted. A few have jobs but are on the brink of losing them. Because gossip and songs have made the neighborhood popular, it costs far more than its moldy ceilings, anemic trees, and high rates of asthma deserve. I don't know how these people keep coughing up the rent.

We have thrown water from the flat roofs of Egypt, where sacred vessels were rinsed. We have roared as marble lions on the war temples of Greece. From English ramparts we have seen necks swing at the gallows, shoulders run red under the lash. In Paris, a million postcards perch us cutely on Notre Dame. In Freiburg, one of our number defecates upon the cornice of the Munster, his crude pose revenge by a fifteenth-century mason upon the nobleman who refused to pay him.

There is a belief, passed down through the centuries, that gargoyles ward off evil. Our monstrous faces must surely be enough to panic the toughest phantom. Churches and minsters, cathedrals, the odd vicarage—we're presumed to defend them from the noxious oils massing round their spires, the midnights waiting to pry with yellow claws their stained vents of glass.

But I am here to tell you: we do not protect.

Our job is not that at all.

You can tell somebody died in here, observes the mother, because it has that shiver feeling.

The father says, Be grateful. It knocked a shit ton off the rent.

People are squeamish, says the mother.

Could we not afford it if she didn't die? asks the daughter.

Jesus, morsel, it's not as if we killed her. The father circles the small rugless room, massaging his bony forearms. This god-damn skin-jacket, I want it off! Why can't I be made of water?

Because you crimed in your last life, says the mother.

Next life we'll be water? asks the daughter.

If you keep on being good. The mother pushes her glass at the girl. Refill my snowbroth, please?

The shame collector lives with his cat, Sophie, who happily does not need to be walked. He has stopped going outside alto-gether. Food comes on bicycles, and toilet paper is mailed from a recycling company. I twist the dial on his radio: explosion here, pile of dead there. The collector, pinning a hemorrhoid to a sheet of foam board, listens for a few seconds, then reaches to turn it off.

•

Into her beloved's room, across the narrow courtyard, the watcher can look with no other hindrance than curtains so flimsy it does not matter whether he draws them. Through her binoculars she sees him wipe his eye, examine the speck, cough.

Look up, she thinks. Look up.

If she had a cat, she would stoop to stroke it. If she had a cat, it would not be a cat but a shark.

The watcher's flat has three windows, two of them boarded. The one in the bathroom is too high and small to nail anything across. She once taped a sheet of construction paper over it, but moisture from her baths made the tape curl off the wall.

A shark, she knows, is not practical as a pet.

Tourists shield upcast eyes from the new-millennium sun, through split fingers see us crouched and leering on parapets, and think *Such quaint remnants!* We remain, to them, from darker, stupider days. It does not occur to these squinters that no days were ever darker than theirs. One glance at a gargoyle and they think *Medieval superstition, how charming* but fail to heed the omens of now: a moron grinning into a microphone, ten-year-old soldiers lined up to march, flags cracking in the desert wind.

In America I have learned the meaning of *heads in the sand*.

Under the watcher's binocular gaze, the beloved and his sidekick recline with beers.

How's your new script going? inquires the sidekick.

Crazy.

Yeah?

As in, crazy-awesome!

What's the plot?

It's a porno about Helen Keller.

Huh. Sounds. . . .

Awesome?

Is Helen Keller an actual character, or is it more like role-play?

The beloved puffs a palm-kiss at the sidekick. More shall be revealed!

I have not yet heard the young one's name spoken. She is referred to simply as *morsel*. She is the only child in the building. Her stockings are red with white rabbits stitched at the knee. I'm sorry, she says daily, for talking too loud when her parents' heads are killing them. When their heads are not killing them, they debate philosophy—of a sort. Theirs is a rather personal metaphysics. They talk of people who have wronged them, fortunes that have skipped them, the various piques and umbrages scattered in their wake. It seems the world has not dealt them a fair hand.

The father reasons, Assholes are not suddenly—or actually, ever—going to vanish from the earth. So the best defense is Hypnos.

Don't forget Morpheus, says the mother.

Since the walls at Leopard Arms are as thick as thick fingernails, shame breeds like a grateful spore.

The collector worries that his snoring will keep the watcher awake. He moved his bed to the far wall, but the room is so narrow not much can be done to impede the travel of his slurpings and honkings and cuh-cuh-*cuchhh*-ings into the adjoining flat. If he sees the watcher in the lobby or hall, he swivels right round. The only mammal who is ever going to sleep next to him, he figures, is Sophie.

Mrs. Megrim, meanwhile, wonders if the flautist hears her crying after short, unsatisfying phone calls with her children. Or if her heavy tread bothers the phantom-faced boy below. Oh, but let him be bothered, she always reminds herself. *Let* him.

The watcher listens to the morsel's parents intercoursing nightly between eleven-fifteen and eleven-thirty, directly under her bed. (The floors are holey.) When softly the tiny sighs begin, the watcher readies herself: face down, toes braced, hips arched, fingers slitted. Sighlets give way to whimpers, a moan or two, then many moans, accelerating. In due course the father joins in with his staccato whinnies. The watcher herself makes no sound.

The tellies switch on by themselves to the news channels. How the fuck, says everybody. The news reveals only a fraction, but that's more than my humans want to hear. Limbs torched, bullets bouncing. Stop looking at that, orders the mother of the morsel, whose eyes are huge at women sobbing round a coffin.

They have no idea I encourage their midnights, rather than frighten them away.

For that, you see, is the gargoyle's way with worry.

We invite.

I am rained on, wind-whipped, scorched. The stone they cut me from was not of high quality, and down the years I have greened and softened. At the academy they drilled us in the history of weather, since we were to live in it. I learned that the ancient Greeks believed truffles were made by thunder: during a storm, the noise would invert itself and sink—newly solid—into fungal soil. The ancient Romans reported that blood and milk poured from the sky, as did iron. And wool. And flesh. Then, of course, cyclones: a notorious peril to seafarers. The nautical remedy was to splash vinegar on the ship before the cyclone's arrival. (Was this effective? The logbooks are unclear.)

My favorite weather is cloud; it reminds me of home. When vapors from the sewage plant waft south to flour the skies, I am, in my way, smiling.

If that child bangs on the wall one more time while my stories are on, I will contact the law.

Oh really? says the mother. And which law would that be?

Mrs. Megrim looks the mother up and down, her mouth a venom bloom. She says, You're so thin it's like a concentration camp happened.

Thank you!

Not a compliment, says Mrs. Megrim.

Actually, says the mother.

The father stops to examine a typed notice affixed to the front door. He is a slow reader. Huh, he says finally, shouldering his sack of bottles.

The new referendum requires all persons over the age of thirty-five to evacuate the neighborhood on or before March 15. Furthermore, per an auxiliary proviso, all persons between eighteen and thirty-five must report to the post office and receive an Appearance Assessment. If deemed inferior for any reason (understyled, overweight, etc.) the person must leave the zip code within sixty days.

Safe for now, says the father, although in a few years we'll be—

Fucked, nods the mother.

The daughter asks, But what if you don't pass the Assessment?

Are you kidding? *Look* at us.

The morsel looks.

The mother says, We're hot, okay?

The only people in the building over thirty-five are Mrs. Megrim and the flautist, who says cheerily, At least they gave us plenty of time to pack!

The referendum can screw, says Mrs. Megrim.

She's been at Leopard Arms since her husband was alive. Together they saw a lot of life pass through these doors. They played rummy here. They bemoaned their children's unwise choices here. They walked across the light-strung bridge after suppers in Manhattan, glad to return to the quiet of here.

I budge not, she declares.

The flautist whispers, They'll come for you eventually.

The watcher's beloved is one of the ones who never go outside. He does his work at home where the sun can't get him. His face is the coldest white, much like those of eighteenth-century women who ate arsenic wafers to bleach their skin. (The arsenic killed the hemoglobin in their blood, and the women grew pale as spiders living on the floor of the sea.)

The beloved reaches the world through his machine. Upon his ashen cheeks, at all hours, jumps blue breath from the screen. He sends reports, receives instructions, unbuckles his belt and digs one hand down to pump while the bodies topple from position to position.

When this latest war started, the academy upped the number of trainees it sent to America. We are sorely needed in the land of the green mermaid. Other places, people are forced to reckon with their midnights because they're standing right in front of them, often holding a rifle. Not so in a country where you can choose, instead of rifles, to think about wrinkle-fighting injections or celebrity custody combat.

During a previous war, slightly to the east of this one, I was fresh-eared at the academy. I couldn't wait to be a dragon on a pagoda, watching gunfire like a cricket match. But my instructor assigned me to the United States.

Shouldn't I go to where the wounded are? I protested.

If you want the blossom to grow, said my instructor, it won't do much good to water the petals. The roots of this suffering are in America. To help the people who are being bombed, you have to go to the nightmare's source.

To his foam display board the collector nails a skinny white leg flecked with golden, girlish hairs.

There are three types of Antarctic penguin, says the morsel.

Is that right, says the father.

King, macaroni, and jackass.

They taught you the word jackass at school?

No, I read it just myself. The king penguin is the size of a goose.

Have you ever *seen* a goose? demands the father. Shit, the fact is, we've never taken you to the zoo. Wife! he hollers at the kitchen.

The macaroni is smaller, continues the morsel, with a white throat.

What about the jackass?

They make a noise like a donkey. And have tiny flippers.

We need to figure out where the zoo is!

The mother stands in the doorway, biting the lip of her glass. But did you see about that kid who got mauled by the

Siberian tiger last month? *Through* the bars, she adds. I think he might've died of his injuries.

The biggest midnight sniffing for the mother is fear—which, of course, is every human's midnight, but for her it assumes an age-old guise: fear of the morsel coming to harm because she, the mother, did not take good enough care of her. Tuberculosis, speeding truck, Siberian tiger: so much could happen.

The father is scared of doing nothing they'll remember him for. Not a single footprint—film, book, record, madcap stunt—to prove he was here. *Am* I actually here? he sometimes mutters into his hand.

Significant fears to face, I would say; but these two do a bang-up job of not. Their evasion strategy is deftly honed. They sleep half the day, snarled up in each other's arms; the other half they drink snowbroth. Eating is not high on the priority list. Their daughter, in fact, seems to be the only cook in the house. What sauce you want on your eggs, Dad? Hot or plum?

They are practically impervious!

Well, it's my job to thwart blitheness. To keep drawing the midnights up from the caves, no matter how slippery these two might be.

I'm not sure what my obligation is to the young one. At what age should a person start being visited by eye-opening discomfort? Our instructors didn't teach us a great deal about children. I think I will leave her alone for now. She already has her parents to cope with, after all.

The watcher and her beloved happen to cross the lobby at the same moment.

She emits a gurgling scream.

He says uneasily, Whut up?

Oh!

Huh?

Hi, she corrects herself.

He nods and hurries out the door. She stands still for several minutes, listening to his voice—three dazzling syllables—play back, play back.

As the sun drops behind the scaffolds of a half-built high-rise, the mother returns from a rare day out. Mrs. Megrim, sitting guard, sees her spit gum onto the sidewalk.

Pick it up! she yells.

The mother walks faster.

Megrim stands with difficulty and arranges her bulk against the door, blocking entry.

Are you kidding? says the mother, adjusting her sunglasses.

I kid not.

Look, I need to get upstairs. I've had this tampon in since seven A.M.

Pick it up off the ground! says Megrim.

It's not *on* the ground, it's in my cunny, growing lethal bacteria.

You want somebody to slip on that? Pick it up, dirty!

I had two job interviews today. Move out of my effing way.

Not until you fetch your effing garbage and stop expecting the world to be cleaned for you.

Not strong enough to shove her aside, the mother stomps back to retrieve the wad.

The shame collector's grandmother has taken to ringing several times a day. When he answers, she does nothing except breathe and fidget; then, before hanging up, she whispers: Poop.

He imagines her in the assisted-living facility, next to a jar of plastic flowers, fretting fruit-bar wrappers in her speckled hands. So he picks up every time, even though the sight of the Florida area code sends a blade into his lung.

How you doing, Nanna? he murmurs, pinning to his board a lame joke he told at the Halloween party.

The flautist departs well before the deadline. A great excuse to travel, she remarks to Mrs. Megrim. I'm going on a singles cruise!

Decent, nods Megrim. But you're still a weakling.

A shark would not be practical, knows the watcher. The tank alone would take up the whole flat, even if she could find someone willing to install it.

He stirs milk on a low flame. According to her logbook, he likes milk to be hot and weather to be cold. He likes cereal to have marshmallows and women to be drunk. Ten-thirty is his preferred hour to rise.

Look up, she whispers. Look up.

Look up because here I am.

There is a lot about the beloved that the watcher can't know. Such as that he spikes that milk with mock absinthe. Such as that he doesn't even own a mattress, and sleeps on a sleeping bag full of twigs and dirt. This girl is really getting the short end of it—in love with deadly marine beasts and writers of smut! I ache to expose him. But that would be solving her pain for her. We are not trained to give them shortcuts.

Agape at his screen, he squeals into the phone, Smoke these subject headings, chap! *Kaela gets laid by her horses. Jalisa sucks off her cows.* It's more or less poetry! *Average moms open their legs for you.*

157

You don't have a junk-mail filter? demands his sidekick.

I don't *want* one, because this poetry's going straight into Helen Keller.

Sunlight enters the body through the eyes, so the residents of Leopard Arms, dark-glassèd whenever they step out, do not get enough vitamin D. Even the morsel is forced to wear red plastic contraptions that make her look like a miniature-golf docent.

A lack of D causes rickets in the young, osteomalacia in the older. Is the morsel walking knock-kneed? When she came home from school yesterday, I noticed a hint of a limp. Could her bones be turning to jam?

At the academy, where we train before manifesting as architecture, they are very firm on one point: *Do not sympathize.* You will think these humans are hapless, indeed pathetic. Do not give in! They must tackle some truths. Confront a few facts. If you let them lead lives of carefree denial, of callous fun-seeking, the race will self-destruct even sooner than it's scheduled to.

Although, chuckled one of my instructors, scratching the horn that left his right eye in shadow, that wouldn't be such a bad thing, now would it?

We baby gargoyles tucked behind our desks giggled too, but nervously. The job seemed massive—beyond our gift.

The little morsel taps on 5-C, palms flat on the sticky door to keep from falling. She is wearing her new skates, smuggled out of the lost-and-found by a teacher who took pity.

The collector answers, holding a box of adhesive strips worn across the bridge of the nose to reduce snoring. They have just come in the post and he wants to practice before night. Yes?

Will you please come watch me skate because I'm not allowed to alone?

Wull. . . .

Because I could get hit by a car or abducted or also killed.

Can't you ask your mom?

She's still asleep.

What about—

He is too.

The collector looks at his watch, raises an eyebrow. Sophie throbs at his ankles.

So can you?

Wull. . . . He is nauseous at the prospect of showing his face in public.

Please? Her rabbity knees are twitching.

He sighs. No, I can't.

The morsel nods.

I'm sorry, I just—

That's okay, she says.

At dawn on March 15, the old emerge from their homes. Some are whisked into the cars of impatient relatives; others lurch by themselves into taxis. Once the sun is up, the rest of the banished start making their way. They pile crates and boxes, picture frames and cacti, into borrowed vans. They push laden shopping carts toward the bridge. They glance wistfully at the new coffee shop/handmade jeans boutique/gym but cry, Fuck this neighborhood anyway. Asthma's not on my Christmas list!

Mrs. Megrim watches the exodus from behind her curtains, shaking her unusually large head.

The morsel has been hurting at the back of her mouth.

You probably just drank something too hot, says the mother.

I was scalded?

Yes you were. Get a piece of ice.

The almonds of her throat are aflame. If anyone were to look, they'd see a raw red swelling. Nobody looks.

A Complete Guide to Hazardous Marine Life contains a photograph of the shark she pines for: not a big shark, only a few feet, but beautiful. Brave. She has peered into its tiny eye a thousand times, even pressed her binoculars up to the page, trying to see to its heart. A shark would defend the watcher from the loneliness I have called upon her. Loneliness, according to our instructors, is among the worst of midnights. It is not a flashy problem like crack, nor easily sympathized for, like cancer. Instead it works slowly up your spine, taking sips of the fluid.

The tour guide exclaims, As you may have guessed from the cute foot traffic, this area has finally been cleared of erstwhilers. Local representatives have been trying to pass an age-and-beauty law for several years and were at last triumphant, making the neighborhood the most enviable address in the entire—

Too bad *you* cannot live here, observes a tourist.

Excuse me?

Well, you are no spring turkey.

The guide's eyelids flutter, but he contains himself. Now then, if you will crane your necks to the left. . . .

On the third day of tonsillitis, the morsel requests a visit to the doctor and is told, Do you think *insurance* suddenly fell from the ceiling?

Pocketing house key and pink wallet, she strides off toward the high street. Returns with a lemon, a radish, and a thick yogurt made in Iceland. She squats over a patch of dirt from which climbs a spindly tree, digging until she finds her quarry.

I'm sorry, she whispers, and chops off the earthworm's head with her key.

Please do not eat that.

If only I had a voice she could hear!

Where is Megrim? Watching her stories, of course. Damnit, Mrs., you are needed.

The tonsil-poultice, pestled in a plastic cup from a hamburger restaurant, is one part radish, two parts worm, and three parts polar curd. Delicious, she whispers staunchly. The parents, heads on fire in the next room, can't hear.

The watcher scratches on the wall above her bed, in black pen: Love is when a thin flame flies under your skin.

Two floors below, across the courtyard, the beloved halts in midpump. He is wincing, not in carnal pleasure but in ordinary pain.

Fuck my back kills!

One can only hope that the twines and tissues of his lumbar are disintegrating, thanks to insufficient vitamin D, a little more each day.

I learned a new thing at recess, croaks the morsel. Want to see?

Stupid with snowbroth, they nod.

She laces her fingers and clamps her fists together. Here is the church, here is the steeple, open the doors and unload clips into the people.

Ha! says the mother.

Do it again, says the father.

In America I have learned the meaning of *last straw*.

Do not try to save them, warned the instructors. One may only teach lessons—never rescue.

But I've been in this country long enough to know that you

can do anything if you just try hard enough and don't ask the government for enfeebling handouts.

I thereby climb out from under the wet blankets of the British Empire and pledge: I *will* rescue.

Not yet sure exactly how.

Oh-em-gee, chap, were you aware that *Pete's mom is ready for hard-core action after some beers?* Or that *crazy farm women are screwing in the barn?* A lot goes on in agricultural settings.

Helen Keller didn't live on a farm, did she?

Sure she did, says the beloved. A farm of the mind.

Nanna, says the collector, did you know that my transformation into a shut-in reeking of cat pee is almost complete?

Breathing.

I haven't left the apartment in a month, he says.

Rustling.

Literally, he adds.

Poop, she says.

Across the water from their horned wisdom, I am betraying my instructors. Merely to entertain the *idea* of rescue is in flagrant defiance of the gargoyle's mission. We are to nudge humans out of their nests, not weave new ones for them.

I can't think of a way to reach her. Not directly. I must act by proxy, entrust the salvage to a go-between.

Hoarse and feverish, the morsel decides to keep herself home from school. The sight of her alarms the parents when they rise at noon.

What the eff? says the mother. It's not the weekend! And what's that smell?

I can't talk, writes the morsel on a take-out menu, *so I am making some cookies.*

Right ho, says the bewildered father.

My powers are limited, but they are powers.

A grain, a grain, a grain.

(I haven't concentrated this hard since my leaving exams at the academy.)

From these grains, be gone all sweetness!

(My stone eyes ache.)

From this cupful, leach all music, expunge all hue, until the cup is sand.

Charity's legs are spread on the ranch! shrieks the beloved, hunched pantless at his screen.

The watcher can see he is excited, and wishes she knew what his words were; she imagines them as little flowers of anguish. *If I had a shark, I could ride it across the yard and through his window and then—*

Oh dear girl, you couldn't.

A knock. Soft, insistent. The beloved debates whether to answer, then—because he's bored—steps into his corduroys. The watcher loses sight of him when he moves for the door.

What are you selling these for?

Only five mere dollars, she whispers.

No, I mean, what organization?

The morsel shrugs.

I'm not paying if I don't know. You could be raising funds for the U.S. Army.

It's for my dad and my mom, rasps the morsel.

They're making you hawk baked goods for personal gain?

They're not making me. I thought of it just myself. They need some money.

But you can't—I mean, that's just *not done*.

I'm doing it, points out the morsel.

Would you like to buy some delicious cookies?

She dangles the ziplock bag with its freight of charred lumps. What flavor?

Oatmeal. Just five dollars only. You can try one for free.

The collector munches contemplatively. This is far from delicious, he says.

The morsel blinks.

In fact it tastes like crap.

He bends to feed the other half to Sophie.

The morsel stares at her thumb.

Did you follow the recipe? he asks, nearly kindly.

I'm pretty sure, whispers the morsel.

I suspect that *sugar* is an ingredient you overlooked.

No, I'm pretty sure.

I advise you to whip up a new batch before you go on peddling your wares.

Here it is. The moment. Please let it succeed, my stratagem, my dicey ploy! I don't pray, because who to? but I concentrate my very hardest.

The old woman reaches into the ziplock, brings a black chunk to her mouth. *What will she say?*

This is nastiness. I wouldn't pay a dime, much less five dollars.

I'm sorry, croaks the morsel.

Never apologize, says Megrim briskly. Just make more.

I don't have more ingredients.

Megrim crunches her mouth into an almost-smile. Well guess who does?

I am embarrassed to feel so wildly relieved. It hardly befits a creature of my station. But her swollen little almonds—and the steeple—and the bloody broth—it simply would not answer.

Mrs. Megrim hands the morsel a wedge of butter wrapped in paper towel. Grease away!

The assiduous child sets to her pans while Megrim beats the dough. The heating oven (seldom cleaned) fills the kitchen with ghosts of ancient suppers.

They sent a needle down his throat, explains Megrim, to find out what ailed his ticker. But while they were doing it, he died. Right on the goddamn table. The needle must've hit something else.

That's so bad, whispers the morsel.

Yeah, it was. It was the worst thing of all.

I wish that didn't happen.

Well, thank you, says Megrim.

Mature ladies showing nasty tricks, mutters the beloved.

Mrs. Megrim has donned her best dress, a blue silk her husband gave her. Too big for it now, she has slashed vents in the back and sides, through which surge rolls of petticoated flesh. In the bathroom mirror she dabs on lipstick. The morsel admires its color, the lit-up brown of raisins. She asks can she have some too and is told to dream on.

My nephew is a doctor in the Bronx, states Megrim, and we're paying him a visit. He'll tell us whether those tonsils need to come out. Here, put on your rag.

165

My pretty coat, corrects the morsel.

I'm sorry, but that hardly adds up to a coat. Wrap this around your neck.

What is it?

My people call it a scarf, says Megrim.

Do you think my mom is beautiful?

Well, ha, well, I—just look at you! Could a child so handsome have come from a nonbeautiful mother?

What is your favorite place on Earth you've been to in real life?

The Bering Strait. On my honeymoon.

What was your favorite thing to make your kids for dinner?

Hot dogs. They had low standards.

And what is the leopard's name?

Henh?

Our leopard.

You mean that fellow above the door?

Yeah him.

My name is

Search me.

But my name is

Doesn't have one, concludes the girl.

Are we done with this interrogation or what?

The morsel hesitates. The question she wants most to ask is not polite. But her worry that Mrs. Megrim is going to leave—a new black dot on her heart—eclipses all else.

Aren't you scared, she blurts, of getting arrested for being not young and then have to move away?

Megrim cackles. No, hon, they won't catch me. I know the tunnels.

I can smuggle food into a tunnel, says the morsel.

That'd be decent.

I'll bring you eggs! And also sandwiches!

Quit shouting, or a rawhead will come for you in the night.

What does one look like?

So hideous, says Megrim, it can't be described.

The crone may know the tunnels, but *I* know what the Evacuation Enforcement Inspectors look like. And upon them I shall invite amnesia, whenever they approach.

The bus is passing once again. I have the spiel, of course, by heart. But today the tour guide strays from his script—he points the microphone at me.

Me?

Has it dawned on them, perchance? Am I about to receive, for the first time, some credit for my work on humans' behalves? I don't need applause (we were trained to expect none) but I wouldn't kick a bit of acknowledgment out of bed. The watcher, for instance, could have thanked me for whisking her out of Leopard Arms and thereby away from the most futile infatuation on record. All it took was a gentle prodding of the Enforcement Inspectors. She had never gone to the post office for her Appearance Assessment, and when they knocked on her door, they found that all was not garden-fresh in Denmark. The girl's skin puts one in mind of stucco, and her hair hasn't felt a grooming product since before the war.

While she waited for the moving van, clutching her stuffed great white, she might have raised her eyes and smiled. She did not.

The shame collector's gratitude did not exactly runneth over, either, despite the lengths I went for him. I got word of the animal clinic, did I not, in one of my brothers' buildings, wherein works a lovely deaf veterinarian? And I tempted the feline ague upon Sophie, did I not? And the collector now has an ice-cream date for next weekend. But there has been no appreciative wink for me, only his jaw at his knees.

In that urine-colored building, announces the guide, is where Brosef Killick wrote the screenplay for *Mount Saint Helen,* which has recently been wowing special-interest audiences across the country. According to my sources, he still lives here, though one might reasonably ask: why not relocate to Tinseltown, Brosef? ·

You mean he's in there right now? coo the passengers.

Quite possibly so.

Fuckin *'ell!* An evident fan stands up and waves frantically. Hey, Killy! Down 'ere! Show us some dingle!

Please take your seat, says the guide.

The voice, whose lost aitches spark in me a blurred nostalgia for home, gets worse. Look out yer window, you tosser!

A window opens and Mrs. Megrim's enormous head pokes forth. Shut that pie-hole!

You shut it, granny.

She withdraws, only to return with a rose-lidded bowl. I'll show you shut it! she screams, hurling the bowl. She's brawny for a woman of her years: the pottery soars all the way to the bus (narrowly missing the Killick enthusiast) and shatters on the upper deck. A little beach of sugar unfurls at their feet.

Nice throw, says the morsel. Elbows propped on the sill, she leans her head against the formidable bicep. Her cheeks are cherrier, thanks to the protein and vegetables she has been ingesting regularly at Megrim's kitchen table.

The tour guide gawks up, shocked to see such an over-age human loose in the neighborhood. Jesus, he murmurs, I thought they got rid of them all.